D1075111

Books by Linell Smith

MOLLY'S MIRACLE

MIRANDA AND THE CAT

THE AUCTION PONY

The Auction Pony

The
Auction
Pony

by Linell Smith

Illustrated by
PEGGY BACON

Little, Brown and Company
Boston   Toronto

jSm 60a

*Published simultaneously in Canada
by Little, Brown & Company (Canada) Limited*

PRINTED IN THE UNITED STATES OF AMERICA

To Louise, to Carter,
and to Severn Chief
with thanks

1

NICKY THOUGHT SCHOOL would never end. He tried hard to forget what day it was and what he would be doing when he got home that afternoon. But the minutes just seemed to drag by. His teacher, Miss Parsons, was surprised that he was so slow in answering the questions she asked him. At last she said in an exasperated tone, "What is the matter with you today, Nicky Davis? Don't you feel well?" His friend Janie Salter, who sat at the desk ahead of him, waved her hand violently.

"Yes, Jane?" said Miss Parsons.

"Nicky's going to the pony sale tonight, Miss Parsons," said Janie breathlessly, "and his father said that he could buy a pony. I guess he's excited about that."

Miss Parsons smiled. "Well, Nicky," she said, "I suppose that I'll have to make some allowances for you, then.

I suppose it's hard to keep your mind on your schoolwork under the circumstances. But I'll expect you to be extra good at your lessons on Monday."

"Yes, ma'am, I will," breathed Nicky gratefully. The bell rang at last. Nicky and Janie grabbed their books and raced out of the building to the school bus. They climbed aboard and made their way back to the last seat. They were always the last children to leave the bus, since they lived farthest from the school. Their parents' farms adjoined one another, and they had been close friends since they were very small.

"Do you think your mother will let you go with us to-night?" asked Nicky as he settled himself down for the long ride ahead.

"Yes, she said it was all right," replied Janie.

"Great," said Nicky. "Dad said we have to leave at six so we can look at the ponies before the sale begins. Suppose we pick you up then."

"Swell," said Janie. "What kind of pony are you going to get, Nicky — some special sort or just a pony?"

"A Welsh mare," replied Nicky, "if we can afford it."

"Ooh," breathed Janie, "Welsh ponies are beautiful. But they are sort of little. You wouldn't be able to ride it very long."

"I know," said Nicky, "but what I really want to do is to have a herd and raise them some day. You know, like Grandfather. He had some of the best Welsh in the East till he got sick and had to sell them all. He's going to help me pick mine out tonight."

Just then the bus halted at Janie's mailbox and she scrambled out of her seat. "See you at six," she called as she skipped off down the dusty road, her book bag and pigtails swinging gaily.

When Nicky reached his own house, he saw an old green car parked near the barn. "Grandfather's home!" he exclaimed, and he ran up the porch steps and into the cool hall. "Grandfather!" he called excitedly. "Where are you?"

"Right here, Nicholas, right here," said a voice from the kitchen, and Nicky dashed through the door. His mother was sitting at the big kitchen table, shelling peas, and beside her sat his grandfather, who was picking out the littlest peas that were the sweetest and popping them in his mouth. "Honestly, Father," laughed Mrs. Davis, "I won't have any left for dinner if you eat them as fast as I shell them."

"Sorry, Amanda," said Grandfather with a twinkle. "The rest are safe, I promise you. Nicky is here now, and he and I have to go over a *very* important matter."

He got up from the kitchen stool. "Come into the parlor, Nicky," he said, "and let's put our heads together over this list."

He stumped into the little room that was never used except for special company. Nicky followed breathlessly at his heels. The blinds were drawn against the western sun and the room looked dim and secret. Nicky's grandfather seated himself on the stiff horsehair sofa and motioned Nicky to sit beside him. Then he pulled a booklet from his pocket. "These are the sales entries," he said.

Nicky looked at the booklet. The cover said *Maryland Spring Pony Sale*. He leafed through it. There were one hundred entries. Each pony was described, and if it was a purebred, its pedigree was given. As he turned a page his eye caught a large red check beside the name of a pony. He stopped and looked up. "Is this one you like, Grandfather?" he asked.

"Nicholas," said his grandfather, in a very serious tone, "if you are high bidder on this little mare, you can consider yourself in the Welsh pony business."

Nicky looked at the page again. *Elbereth Guinevere*, it read, *gray mare, 12 years old, by Elbereth Geraint out of Fells Marchioness. In foal to Elbereth Gawain. Due to foal by sales time.*

"Do you know her, Grandfather?" he asked.

"I bred her," replied Grandfather simply.

"Is she pretty?" asked Nicky.

"She was one of the loveliest fillies it has ever been my fortune to see," replied Grandfather. "As luck would have it, I had my heart attack the year after she was foaled. I must say, I am curious to know why she has changed hands so much. I've never heard of the fellow that owns her now and I know for a fact that she has been sold at least twice before. Now, how much can you spend for the pony?"

"Three hundred dollars," said Nicky.

"Hm," said Grandfather. "She should be worth a sight more than that — but you never know."

Just then Nicky's father put his head in the door. "Everybody ready for supper?" he asked. "There's a date we have to keep at six, you know."

When supper was over, Nicky said, "Janie wants to come, and I told her we'd take her. Is that all right, Pop?"

"Sure thing," said his father. "Give her a call now and tell her we'll pick her up at the end of her lane in about five minutes."

Nicky did as he was told and then joined his father and grandfather in the Harrises' van that they had borrowed for the occasion. When they picked up Janie, the two children got in the back of the van.

"It's fun riding in here," said Janie.

"It would be more fun if there were a pony riding with us," said Nicky.

"Well, maybe there will be tonight," said Janie.

"I hope it's Guinevere," said Nicky. Then he told her about his talk with Grandfather before supper.

When they got to Timonium Fairgrounds, where the sale was to be held, they found that there were quite a few other prospective buyers who had come early to look over the stock.

They started down the aisles of the horse barns. Nicky

had never seen so many ponies. There were ponies of all sizes and shapes and kinds. It seemed to Nicky as he passed stall after stall that all the ponies in Maryland must be here. At last Grandfather said, "Ah, here we are," and they stopped beside a box stall at the end of the second barn. Nicky peeped through the bars in the door. In the far corner of the stall stood a silvery-colored little mare. How wild and frightened she looked, he thought. Her forelock streamed over her face, almost hiding her large dark eyes, and her silver tail swept the ground. On her hip was her sales number — 33. "Can't see too much in the stall," said Grandfather. "Let's find her owner and ask him to take her out for us."

At that moment a large red-faced man appeared. He hung a lead shank by the stall door and was about to disappear again when Grandfather said, "Pardon me, sir, but can you tell my grandson and me anything about this pony?"

The man looked Grandfather over carefully. Then he said, "This is a grand little mare. Very well bred indeed."

"Really?" said Grandfather innocently. "Well, I'm sure that's very nice. But you see, this pony has caught my grandson's eye and I would like to know if she would be suitable for a child. Any bad habits — that sort of thing."

The red-faced man looked away for a moment and then said, "Well, now, she's got some of the best blood in the country and is due to foal within the week to a top stallion."

"Oh," said Grandfather thoughtfully. Then he said, "I don't suppose you could bring her out for the boy to see?"

A funny look passed over the man's face. He hesitated a minute but then said, "Sure thing, sure thing."

He picked up the shank and moved to the stall door. "Stand back, sonny," he said to Nicky. "This little gal has been running out all her life and isn't much used to people."

He went into the stall cautiously, holding the shank behind his back. Guinevere huddled into the darkest corner of the stall and eyed the intruder fearfully. Suddenly, as he approached her, she came to life. She dashed toward the stall door, almost knocking the man down in her effort to get past him. However, he jumped out of the way and grabbed her halter as she went by. Then, after snapping on the shank, he led her from the stall.

Luckily Grandfather and Nicky were standing well back by this time, for the little mare really put on a show. Though hampered by the weight of her unborn foal, she tried every trick in the book to get free. Nicky stood with his mouth open while the silver mare reared and spun, her owner shouting at her in anger. When Nicky stole a glance at Grandfather he was startled to notice a bright gleam of amusement in the old man's eyes and a look of satisfaction on his face. It disappeared almost at once as he said in a horrified tone, "Does she always behave like that? She seems quite dangerous to me."

The red-faced man was puffing by now. He gave the shank a vicious jerk. "She's a little upset," he said. "Strange place and all — she's just not used to it." He finally pulled the frantic pony back to her stall by brute force and closed the door.

Grandfather stood shaking his head doubtfully. "Don't think I'd trust a child with that pony," he murmured.

"Oh," blustered her owner, "she's a grand little mare, a

grand little mare. Don't know what got into her just now. She's not like herself at all."

"Hm," said Grandfather. "Well, Nicky, let's go look at some of the other animals and see if we can find one you like as well that would be more suitable. Thank you very much, sir, for your trouble," he added.

"Not at all," said the red-faced man. "Keep her in mind, now. The little boy would have a very fine pony if he bought this mare."

"Oh, yes indeed," said Grandfather in a rather strange tone. "Come along, Nicholas."

When they were around the corner of the barn, Nicky looked up at Grandfather and saw that he was brimming with silent laughter. Finally when they were well out of earshot he sat down on a bale of straw and laughed until the tears ran down his face. Nicky stared at him in amazement. "What is it, Grandfather?" he asked. "What's so funny?"

Grandfather's laughter subsided and he pulled his handkerchief from his pocket and wiped his eyes.

"I think we may have a chance, after all," he said gaily. "This spring sale is supposed to be for kids' ponies. Why, when she gets in that ring, she's going to act like a wild woman. Most of your bidders won't touch her."

Just then a man passed them leading a hunting pony, beautifully turned out. Its bay coat shone in the failing

light and its mane and tail were faultlessly braided. "Jim!"
cried Grandfather.

The man turned and then advanced with a big smile and
an outstretched hand. "Mr. Stires," he said warmly, "how
are you, sir?"

"Fine, just fine," beamed Grandfather. "Jim, this is my
grandson Nicholas. Nicky, Jim was my right-hand man
when I had the ponies."

"Those were grand times, sir," said Jim, "and a sad day
it was when they had to go. Are you here to watch, or are
you thinking of getting back into the game again?"

"Not me, Jim, but Nicholas here," said Grandfather.
"I'm just his adviser. But I wonder if you might help us
with some information?"

Jim's face broke into a wide grin. "It wouldn't be about
the little gray mare, now would it?" he asked.

Grandfather laughed. "Jim, you know me too well," he
said. "It would indeed. What do you think it will take to
get her?"

Jim considered this for a minute. "Well," he said at last,
"that's hard to say. No one in his right mind would buy
her for a kid's pony, and she's got a bad name with the
breeders too. Can't pasture her safely, you see. She'll jump
anything and it's an awful nuisance to cope with an animal
that's always running off and is difficult to deal with if she's
kept in stable. You might have a sleeper there, Mr. Stires."

Grandfather looked thoughtful. "Thanks, Jim," he said.

"You're welcome, sir, and good luck to you and the lad tonight. I'd like to see that little mare back where she belongs." Jim touched his cap and moved off with the bay pony.

"Well," said Grandfather, "it's just about sales time. We'd best get ourselves a good ringside seat." They entered the sales pavilion and joined Mr. Davis and Janie in seats beside the ring.

Janie said breathlessly, "What was she like?"

"Beautiful," said Nicky dreamily.

"How about it, Mr. Stires," asked Nicky's father. "Has the boy a chance of getting this pony that Janie's been telling me about?"

"Could be," said Grandfather. "The mare's as wild as a deer and that will throw buyers off."

"Is she safe?" asked Mr. Davis.

"I've known enough ponies to say that I believe that if Nicky has patience and determination in dealing with her, he'll have made a lifelong friend in a few months," said Grandfather. "That mare is frightened to death of everything and everyone, and from what I saw of her handling just now, I can't say I blame her."

Just then the first pony was led into the ring, and the Maryland Spring Pony Sale was on.

Nicky was fascinated. He watched as the auctioneer

called for bids and acknowledged them from his various helpers posted at different parts of the arena. "One-fifty, I'm offered one-fifty," the auctioneer would drone. "Who'll make it two?"

"Here," one of the helpers in the ring would signal, and the auctioneer would again urge the price upward.

One of the men in the ring was standing near them now, and Grandfather leaned forward to speak to him. "I'm interested in lot thirty-three for my grandson," he murmured.

"Fine," said the man, "I'll keep an eye on you."

At last, the moment came. "Lot thirty-three," announced the auctioneer. "Welsh mare — Elbereth Guinevere by Elbereth Geraint out of Fells Marchioness. This mare is twelve years old and is in foal to that good stallion Elbereth Gawain. Ladies and gentlemen, this is a well-bred mare and the foal she is carrying should be a dandy. Here's a mare to build a Welsh herd on."

Nicky looked expectantly at the in gate. No pony. People began to crane their necks. Still no pony. Suddenly there was a great commotion. People who had been standing at the gate scattered wildly, and into the arena burst Guinevere, her panting owner pulling frantically at the lead shank. Grandfather's expectations were fully realized. The lights, the crowd, the loudspeaker, all these things threw the pony into a dreadful state of terror and her handler's shouts did little to calm her.

Everyone was hypnotized by the sight of the little silver mare dragging her handler around the ring.

At last the bidding began. "Let's start her at five hundred," said the auctioneer. "Five, five hundred. Who'll give me five hundred?"

Evidently there were no takers. "That's a lot, isn't it?" whispered Nicky fearfully.

"Not for this pony," said Grandfather.

The bidding finally started at fifty dollars and went up quickly to one hundred and seventy-five, where it stuck for a while. The man in the ring, who had been glancing at Grandfather, suddenly called in for two hundred. Nicky had not seen Grandfather make a move. "Was that us?" he whispered.

"Yes," said Grandfather. "Now let's see what happens."

From the opposite side of the ring came "Two-twenty-five!"

"Hang it," muttered Grandfather. "I wish Sam Jackson had stayed in Florida another week."

"Who's he?" asked Nicky.

"Big Welsh breeder, and he breeds darn fine ponies," said Grandfather. "He knows what this mare is worth."

Nicky felt like crying. How could he hope to outbid a big breeder? And he had already lost his heart to the wild little mare.

Again the man in the ring called in Grandfather's bid — two-fifty.

It held for a while, and then "Two-seventy-five!" came from the far side of the ring. Grandfather let this go for some time, while Nicky's heart pounded wildly. At last Grandfather advanced to two hundred and eighty-five. "Three hundred!" from Mr. Jackson.

The tears welled up in Nicky's eyes. He had lost the mare. The ring swam before him. Suddenly "Three-fifty!" was called in, but Nicky hardly heard it. "Three-fifty once," said the auctioneer. "Three-fifty twice. Sold for three hundred and fifty dollars." And the pony was led from the ring.

So that was that. Guinevere was sold to somebody else. Nicky rubbed his eyes to get rid of the unwelcome tears.

"Well," said Grandfather briskly. "I guess we had better go look at our pony."

Nicky stared at him. "Our pony?" he gasped. "But I only had three hundred dollars."

"That's as may be," said Grandfather. "But I had fifty dollars I just didn't know what to do with. So I thought I might as well blow it on a good pony for my grandson."

"Nicky!" squealed Janie. "She's yours! Oh, this is exciting!"

Nicky's father said with a grin, "Well, Mr. Stires, I think we owe you a great big vote of thanks. I was watching Nicky's face when he thought he had lost the pony, and I think I would have gone on with the bidding myself if you hadn't stepped in."

Nicky grabbed Grandfather's hand and tugged. "Come on, Grandfather," he begged. "Let's go find Guinevere."

"Well, there's a little matter that has to be attended to first," said Grandfather. "A matter of three hundred and fifty dollars."

"I'll take care of that," said Nicky's father. "You three go on and I'll meet you at the van."

"Fine," said Grandfather. "All right, children, let's go get the pony we've just bought."

They had no trouble finding Guinevere in the large hall adjoining the sales pavilion. "Just follow our noses to trouble," said Grandfather, "and there she'll be."

He was right. A small crowd was gathered at one end of the hall watching the silver pony rear and struggle to escape its tether. They hurried over. The red-faced man was mopping his brow when they arrived. Nicky heard him say under his breath, "Good riddance to you, you little vixen."

Grandfather presented him with the bill of sale and the man said, "Well, she's all yours, mister."

"She was once," said Grandfather gently. "But now she's my grandson's." He took the mare's lead shank and spoke to her softly. Her tiny ears pricked as she listened to him nervously, ready to leap away at one false move. But gradually the pony relaxed a bit almost in spite of herself.

A voice spoke from the group that was watching. "Making a comeback, David?"

Grandfather answered without looking around. "Sam," he said. "You should have outbid me tonight. You let a good one go."

An elderly man moved forward and glanced at the pony.

"I know it," he said genially. "But what would I have done with her? She'd have to be part of the broodmare band, and yet from what I hear of her she'd lead my boys a merry chase cross-country every day. A mare with no show record behind her can't afford to be a troublemaker. I wasn't going over three hundred. Wasn't going that high, truthfully, till I saw you were bidding."

"For my grandson here," said Grandfather. "Nicholas, this is Mr. Sam Jackson. You'll be seeing a lot of each other this summer."

"How do you do, sir," said Nicky politely.

"Going to come and watch a few shows?" asked Mr. Jackson. "Fine, fine. You can learn a lot that way, young man."

"Oh, we might participate in some," said Grandfather mildly.

Mr. Jackson laughed. "With that wild woman? You always were one for a joke, David."

Grandfather smiled. "Your good mares better look to their laurels, Sam," he said.

Mr. Jackson stared at him. "I believe you're serious," he said.

"I am," said Grandfather. "I'll even make a little wager

with you that you are now looking at the National Champion Welsh Mare for this year."

Mr. Jackson whistled. "You've taken leave of your senses, David," he said, "but I'll take you on. What are the stakes?"

"A free stud service to your Starfire," said Grandfather. "If the mare wins the championship the foal is ours. If she loses, you'll have a top foal."

"Done," said Mr. Jackson, laughing. "I'm afraid, David, that you'll be giving up a real good foal."

"Well, well," said Grandfather. "We'll see." He turned to Nicky and said, "Now we've got a frightened pony to load, Nicky. I think we had better get on with it, for it may take some time." And he started leading Guinevere slowly from the hall with Janie beside him.

"Good-by, Mr. Jackson," said Nicky.

"Good-by, sonny," said Mr. Jackson. "You know, your grandfather is quite a man with ponies, but this time I think he's bitten off more than he can chew."

"Oh, no sir," said Nicky loyally, "Grandfather never does that." He turned and hurried after Grandfather.

Outside in the darkness, far from the noise and turmoil of the sale, was the van. By the time Nicky caught up to Grandfather, he had almost reached it. The ramp was down and Nicky's father was standing beside it holding an envelope. "Here are her papers," he said as they came up.

"Fine," said Grandfather. "Put them in the glove compartment for now, please, Paul. I have a feeling I'm going to need your help in loading."

"Be right with you," said Mr. Davis. He put the envelope in the cab and came back to the ramp.

"Now tell me what you want me to do," he said.

"Nothing — yet," said Grandfather. "I don't want to frighten her if I can help it, so I'll try by myself first. You stand by one of the sides, Paul. Nicky, stand by the other. And Janie, stand behind the pony, please. Not too close, now. That's it. Now, when I move her forward, follow her, Janie. And Nick and Paul, try to keep her from running off to the side of the ramp. All right, let's go."

He started forward, clucking to Guinevere. She followed hesitatingly until she reached the foot of the ramp. Then she stopped and began to tremble. Grandfather spoke to her, quietly urging her on. She rolled her eyes wildly and started to back, but Janie raised her arms suddenly and with a leap Guinevere shot forward up the ramp. Grandfather barely had time to get out of the way. There was a terrific commotion in the van as Grandfather tried to back her into the middle stall. For a while Nicky thought she would never do it, but finally, with Mr. Davis's help, she was backed in. The bar was dropped in place in front of her and the head chains were snapped to her halter.

"Whew," said Grandfather, looking at her appreciatively, "this pony's got a mind of her own."

It was decided that Nicky and Grandfather would ride

in back with the pony. Mr. Davis thought that Grandfather would be more comfortable in front, but Grandfather said, "Paul, there have been very few times in my life when I didn't travel with my ponies. This isn't going to be one of them. I'm a firm believer in responsibility to one's animals. That's why I want Nicky with me. His little mare feels frightened and alone. He is going to learn how to make her feel confident and loved. And he'll only do that by being with her as much as he can."

So the ramp was raised and fastened, and Mr. Davis and Janie got into the cab.

They were off. Nicky's father was a very good driver. The van never jerked or jumped, but still the people in back had their hands full.

Guinevere threw herself against the bar. She struggled desperately to free herself from the head chains.

"We've got trouble, Nicky," said Grandfather in a serious tone. "This pony's about to have a van fit. Ring the bell."

Nicky pushed the emergency bell hard, but the van rolled on. He pushed it again. Still his father did not slow down.

"It doesn't work, Grandfather!" he said in a scared voice. "What'll we do?"

Grandfather hesitated. Then he said, "I've got a wild hunch. Here, take one end of the bar. I'm going to let her loose."

Nicky did as he was told. They dropped the bar and then Grandfather, keeping hold of the lead shank with one hand, undid the chains with the other. As the pony leaped forward he pushed Nicky into one of the stalls.

A strange thing happened. As soon as Guinevere felt herself free she quieted down. Her eyes still rolled and her lip twitched nervously, but she spraddled her legs to brace herself against the swaying of the van and she stood still.

Grandfather gave a sigh of relief. "Well," he said cheerfully, "that's one hunch that paid off."

"Is she quieter because she's freer?" asked Nicky.

Grandfather looked at him approvingly. "She is indeed," he said. "You're getting to know your pony."

"What would have happened if we hadn't turned her loose?" asked Nicky.

"She'd have lost all her sense and gotten on the floor, and she probably would have been hurt very badly and lost her foal in the bargain. A van fit's no fun."

They felt the van slow down and stop to drop Janie off and then they felt it turn into their own road. At last it stopped.

Mr. Davis came round to let down the ramp.

"How did it go?" he called through the door.

"A quiet trip," said Grandfather with a wink to Nicky. "A real quiet trip, Paul."

Whether Guinevere had been subdued by the van ride or whether she had just decided to stop fighting was a question that Grandfather couldn't answer, but she walked down the ramp like a lady and went quietly to the large box stall in the barn.

"Good thing you had that stall," said Grandfather approvingly. "It must be a foaling stall for a draft mare."

"I think it was," said Mr. Davis. "You know old Pat Kelly had Belgians and he lived in this place for years."

"Well, she won't feel too penned up when she's in there," said Grandfather.

He was quite right. The stall was really an aisle of the barn that was boarded off. Nicky had lovingly laid a thick blanket of golden straw on the floor that morning, and Guinevere looked as if she were standing in a sea of bedding. A door at the far end led out to a paddock.

"Perfect quarters," said Grandfather with a smile. "I couldn't have wished for better if I'd built it myself. Now then, Paul, where is the cot?"

"Right here, Mr. Stires," said Nicky's father. As they turned to look, Mrs. Davis came out of the feed room with a smile on her face. "It's all made up for you, Dad," she said, "and I've put the alarm clock and a radio in there too. This is just like old times."

"Cot?" said Nicky. "Grandfather, are you going to sleep down here tonight?"

"I am," said Grandfather. "You've a grand little mare here that's due to foal soon, and she's not going to be alone when she does it."

"Can I stay down with you?" begged Nicky.

"No," said Mrs. Davis. "Grandfather is going to take the night shift, Nicky, and you will watch her tomorrow. Now, dear, will you show me your pony? I haven't seen her yet, you know."

"Oh sure!" said Nicky proudly. He led his mother to the stall. "This is Guinevere, Mom," he said. "Isn't she pretty?"

Mrs. Davis looked at the silver mare and smiled. "You know, I think I know her. Wasn't she foaled at the old place, Father?"

"She was indeed," said Grandfather.

"Well then, Nicky," said his mother, "I know that you've had a stroke of luck. She was your grandfather's pride and joy. He always said that she was the best filly he'd ever seen."

"Say goodnight to her, son," said Mr. Davis. "It's getting late, and tomorrow you'll be on duty, you know."

Nicky opened the stall door and walked in quietly. Guinevere eyed him nervously. He squatted down in the straw with his hand out. In it was a piece of sugar that he had been saving. The little mare took a few steps toward him. She reached out her nose until it almost touched his fingers. For a moment he felt that she would take the sugar, but suddenly she whirled and trotted to the far end of the stall.

Nicky got up with a sigh. "I guess she doesn't know me yet," he said.

"I'd say that you did pretty well for your first try," said Grandfather encouragingly. "That's more than she would have done for her last owner. Now off to bed or you'll be too sleepy to keep a sharp eye out tomorrow."

So Nicky and his father and mother went up to the house. They stayed with him while he got undressed so he could tell them about everything that had happened. At last he was in bed.

"Goodnight, Nick," said his father. "I think you've got a fine pony, son."

"Goodnight, darling," said his mother as she turned off the light. "Sweet dreams."

"Goodnight," murmured Nicky.

2

THE NEXT MORNING dawned bright and warm. Nicky jumped out of bed and scrambled into his clothes. Downstairs, his mother and father were finishing breakfast. " 'Morning, Dad, 'morning, Mom!" said Nicky on his way to the door.

"Just a minute, my friend," said his mother, barring the way. "A little breakfast first, please."

"Oh Mom," groaned Nicky. "I want to see the pony."

"You'll be seeing her all day long," said his mother. "Now eat your breakfast."

Nicky reluctantly did as he was told. At last he was through and he dashed to the barn. There he met Grandfather, who was standing by the stall looking at Guinevere.

"Good morning, Grandfather," said Nicky excitedly. "Has she had her foal yet?"

" 'Morning, Nicholas," said Grandfather. "No, not yet,

but she will very soon now. She's started to wax up. Do you see the little beads of moisture on her teats? That's what we horsemen call wax, although it's really colostrum, which is the first milk. When that wax appears you can generally figure on a mare's foaling in the next twenty-four hours. She may go into labor on your shift. So keep a close watch on her and call me if labor starts."

"But gosh, how'll I know?" asked Nicky.

"She'll act restless," said Grandfather. "Restless and uncomfortable. She might kick or bite at her sides, or get down and roll a bit. If you see her down, call me immediately."

"Okay," promised Nicky.

He waited until Grandfather had left the barn and then let himself into the stall with Guinevere. "I'll clean your stall out," he said to the pony, "and put down a lot of fresh straw so it will be very soft for you and the baby."

Guinevere watched him as he walked through the stall. He opened the door at the far end and the sunlight poured in. Then he got a pitchfork and began forking the manure into a wheelbarrow drawn up to the outside door. Then he pushed it over to the manure pile at the far side of the barnyard, where he dumped it. Guinevere watched all this with keen interest. At last she ventured out of her stall and into the paddock. The grass was green here, and soon she was grazing comfortably, although she kept a wary eye on all of Nicky's movements.

Nicky finished the stall by putting down fresh straw and hay, and cleaning and refilling the water bucket. He looked in the feed bucket and saw that a lot of the grain which Grandfather had fed the pony earlier had been left.

Then he went and sat by the stall door to watch his pony. She looked as lovely to him in the morning as she

had the evening before. He knew enough about the better points of the Welsh to realize that she was something special. She had prominent large dark eyes, a refined little head that was slightly dished and which tapered tremendously at the muzzle. A good neck was set into a powerful, deep shoulder which allowed for the lovely floating action of which she was capable. A wonderfully level top line ended in a gay tail set. And above everything else there was an X quality about her, something that made one look twice. It was almost as if she knew she was something special.

A bumblebee buzzed round Guinevere's ears and she shook her head and stamped. Then she trotted toward the paddock fence. Nicky held his breath. But the pony turned and walked the fence line. She was not in a jumping mood today. Nicky watched her with sympathy as she walked the perimeter of the enclosure, stopping every now and again to gaze at the inviting green fields beyond. "I don't blame you, Guinevere," whispered Nicky. "I wouldn't like to be shut up either."

The mare stared at him for a minute. Then she swung her head around to bite at her flank. She stamped impatiently and trotted to the far end of the paddock.

"Fly must have bitten her," said Nicky to himself. But Guinevere kept trotting. She was starting to sweat now. Nicky got a little worried. "I'd better call Grandfather. I don't know what's the matter, but something is." He turned to run to the house but gave a sigh of relief as he saw Grandfather coming down the road to the barn. "Grandfather," he called, "come quick!"

Grandfather broke into a lope. He reached Nicky in no time and stood beside the boy, watching the pony. Guinevere was galloping in circles by now.

"We'd better get her into the stall," said Grandfather. "I think the foal is on the way."

"Why is she running, though?" asked Nicky.

"All mares are different," said Grandfather. "I guess Guinevere's idea of how to stop being uncomfortable is to run away."

He walked out into the paddock. "See if you can help me herd her into her stall, Nicky," he said.

Between them, they were able to do it, helped perhaps by the fact that Guinevere suddenly remembered the cool stall shaded from the hot glare of the sun and its inviting bed of straw. When they got her inside, Grandfather shut the door and settled down in the straw himself. "Sit down, Nicky," he said, "and keep perfectly quiet now. We don't want to disturb the mare. We just want to be here to help if she needs us."

Guinevere paced restlessly back and forth. Twice she lay down but then got up again. At last she lay down and stretched out full length. "Shouldn't be long now," whispered Grandfather.

In no time at all, it seemed, a new life had arrived in the

[35]

soft straw. Grandfather went quietly over to the mare and her foal. He took a knife from his pocket and cut the cord, then painted the stump with iodine. He pulled the new baby around in front of its mother so she could see her little one and still rest from her recent labor. "We've got a beautiful colt," said Grandfather to Nicky exultantly. "Best I've ever seen. Now then, Mama," he said to the pony, "he's all yours. Take care of him."

But Guinevere, instead of licking her baby dry, seemed just as uncomfortable as ever. She bit at her sides and seemed to strain. Grandfather looked at her quickly and then he said, "Nicky, run up to the house and give Dr. Frock a call. Tell him that I'd appreciate it if he'd get over here as soon as he can. Tell him we've got a mare that's having twins and the second one doesn't seem to be in the right position to get itself born."

"Yes, sir," said Nicky, his eyes wide with fear. As he tore up the road to the house, his mind was in a whirl. Twins — why, mares rarely had them. And when they did it was usually bad luck all around. They practically never survived, and the mare was almost always injured during the birth, and could even die herself.

He barreled into the kitchen, the screen door slamming behind him. His mother stared at him. "What's the matter?" she asked. Nicky was by this time dialing the veterinarian's number. "Twins," he said briefly.

"Oh no!" said his mother, putting down the plate she had been wiping. "Oh, Nicky."

Just then Nicky heard Dr. Frock's voice at the other end of the line. He gave a quick prayer of thanks. Dr. Frock was a very busy man and he was lucky to catch him. "Dr. Frock," he said breathlessly, "this is Nicky Davis. We've got a pony mare foaling and it's twins. There's trouble with the second one. Can you please come?"

"Be right over," said Dr. Frock. "Hold the fort till I get there. I won't be long."

"Gee, thanks," said Nicky. He hung up and started back to the barn. When he got there he saw his mother in the corner of the stall rubbing the first foal with straw. When she saw him she beckoned. "Here, Nicky, you finish drying this little fellow, and I'll go with Grandfather and see if I can help there."

Nicky looked at the foal that lay before him on the straw. He seemed so tiny and helpless. All knees and hocks. He nickered in his brand-new voice. The boy rubbed him briskly with the straw.

Soon the little one started to try out his unruly legs. Nicky had to laugh at his efforts. Either his forelegs or hind legs would buckle, and back down in the straw he would go. Finally he made a very determined effort and got both sets under control. He stood, a bit uncertainly perhaps, but very pleased with himself for all that. Nicky

smiled at him. The foal was so unafraid, so trusting. He
nickered again and whisked his little brush of a tail up and
down. He looked at Nicky expectantly. Nicky put out his
hand and the foal nibbled at his fingers. His muzzle was
velvet-soft and his mouthing didn't hurt at all, for his pink
gums were bare of teeth. "I haven't anything to feed you,"
said Nicky sadly. "We just have to pray your mom will
be okay."

At that moment the veterinarian arrived. Just as he entered the stall, Grandfather said, "Here's the twin." And
the second foal was born. It lay motionless on the straw,
lifeless, it seemed — a tiny shape that drew Nicky's eyes like
a magnet.

Both Grandfather and Dr. Frock gave full attention to
the mare, and Nicky, knowing that she was in the best
hands possible, crept over to the still little body of the
second foal. He lifted its head. The nostrils seemed clogged

with fluid. Suddenly Nicky was filled with determination. This foal *would* live. He would make it live. Feverishly he cleaned the tiny nose, and, opening its mouth, he cleaned that out too. Then he held the muzzle close and breathed into the foal's nostrils. "Please live," he begged. "Oh please, please live!"

It seemed forever that he had been breathing his life's breath into the foal when suddenly the little thing gave an odd gasp. Nicky redoubled his efforts and the foal gasped again. It was breathing on its own! Nicky sat back on his heels for a minute to rest, and savor the wonderful new feeling that came over him. He had helped give life to something. Moments ago, the foal had lain still as death. And now it lived. He had willed it to live. His body filled with exultation and he felt like shouting for joy.

A hand touched his shoulder, and looking up he saw Dr. Frock. "Well, darned if you didn't get the little fellow going," said the doctor with a grin.

"Is Guinevere all right?" asked Nicky anxiously.

"Right as rain," said Dr. Frock cheerfully. "A little pooped, but by tomorrow she should be fine."

Nicky sighed with relief. Grandfather came over and looked down at the second foal, a frown on his face. "What about this one, Doc?" he asked. "Do you think it will pull through?"

"Heck, Dave, I can't tell you that for sure," said Dr. Frock. "Chances are all against it, but you never know. I might as well give him his foal shot same as his brother and a little something extra to liven him up a bit."

Nicky watched as the vet gave both foals their shots. Neither so much as jumped. "Gee!" he thought. "I wish Dr. Frock could give me *my* shots. It doesn't look as if it hurt at all!"

As the grown-ups were busy with the foals, he went quietly over to Guinevere, who lay, breathing softly at last, in the center of the stall. He sat down beside her gently and said, "Good girl, Guinevere. You have two beautiful foals. I helped with one of them. Please, can't we be friends now?" He put out his hand and rested it on her lathered neck. For a moment her eyes shone dark with fear, and then suddenly she gave a sigh and relaxed. Nicky's face broke into a delighted grin. He took some clean straw and began gently to rub the little mare dry, talking to her all the while. At last she closed her eyes and dozed as the boy rubbed her body, easing her tired muscles.

Grandfather watched Nicky with approval. "Well, Nicky," he said at last, "I believe you've made a friend."

"I hope so, Grandfather!" said Nicky fervently. "I do hope so."

Now Grandfather, Nicky, and his mother listened to Dr. Frock's instructions for caring for mother and babies. Guinevere was to get a warm bran mash tonight and to-morrow morning. The foals were to be kept warm and dry and their navels treated with iodine every day. It might be necessary to raise the second foal on a bottle if the mare didn't have enough milk. "Why not let him nurse the mare?" asked Nicky. "He needs her milk the most."

"Because," said Grandfather, "his chances aren't very good anyway. We want to make sure one lives, and the strongest one is our best bet."

"Oh," said Nicky sadly.

"Well, I'll check in tomorrow and see how everyone is doing," said Dr. Frock. "Call me if anything goes wrong between now and then."

"Thanks, Doc," said Grandfather. "It surely was a comfort to have you here. See you tomorrow."

While Mrs. Davis walked back up the road with the veterinarian, Nicky went back to the stall. The first foal was staggering around in the straw, getting the feel of his legs. His twin was still lying quietly under the blanket that had been put over him to keep him warm. Guinevere gave a long sigh and then rose to her feet. She whinnied gently to her active son, who answered in his high little voice. The second foal raised his head and whinnied, too. Guinevere's eyes grew startled. She whirled round and approached him. This was strange to her. She was used to one baby, but two? She blew out her breath in snorts. The foal whinnied again. His mother sniffed him mistrustfully. But his smell reassured her. He was hers, all right, but why wasn't he on his feet? She nudged him gently, insistently. The little creature tried gallantly to respond, but he was too weak. He hadn't the strength to stand.

"Come, Nicky," said Grandfather, after watching the mare's efforts for a moment or two. "Let's see if we can help out a bit."

They re-entered the stall. "You lift the baby and I'll hold the mare," said Grandfather.

Nicky did as he was told. He carefully raised the foal, locking his hands just behind the forelegs, his arms forming a sling. The little one was light as a feather. Carefully, he lifted him over to Guinevere's side. The mare stood quietly

while Nicky guided the foal's muzzle toward her bag. On the other side his twin was sucking greedily. Try as he would, however, Nicky couldn't get the foal to nurse. At last he said to Grandfather, "What'll we do, Grandfather? How can we get him to eat?"

"I'll milk the mare, I guess," said Grandfather. "You go ask your mother if she's got any old baby bottles lying around."

When Nicky returned a little later, bottle in hand, Grandfather had some of the mare's milk in a bucket. He poured it carefully into the bottle and put the nipple on. "Now we'll try him again," he said.

Nicky lifted the foal's head while Grandfather put the nipple into his mouth. But the baby would not or could not suck. Even when, as a last measure, Grandfather cut the top off the nipple and poured the milk into the colt's mouth, it only trickled out the corner. He did not try to swallow.

Grandfather stood up with a sigh. "We've done all we can for now, Nicky," he said. "Why don't you go to the house and clean up. It must be about lunchtime. I'll see that everything's shipshape down here and then I'll be up too."

Nicky said sadly, "Okay, Grandfather, but I hate to leave the baby."

"I know," said Grandfather, "but there are times, Nicky, when we have done all we can, and then we just have to wait and hope."

Nicky nodded and walked slowly from the barn back to

the house. There he found a pleasant surprise. His mother had asked Janie for lunch. She was waiting for him in the kitchen, her eyes wide as saucers. "How are they all?" she asked. "Guinevere and the babies? Your mother told me it was twins."

"Dr. Frock says Guinevere's fine," said Nicky. "And so is the first colt. But," he finished sadly, "the other one won't eat at all."

Nicky and Janie rushed through lunch, and then Nicky said, "Mom — is it okay now if Janie and I go sit with Guinevere and the foals?"

His mother flashed a glance at Grandfather, who had just come in. Grandfather shrugged his shoulders. "Amanda," he said, "they may as well. Growing up can be hard sometimes — but it's got to be done."

When they left the house, Janie asked, "What did he mean, Nicky?"

Nicky was silent for a minute before he answered. Then he said, "Well, I guess he meant that he doesn't think the foal will live and that maybe he'll die when we're with him."

"Oh," said Janie. "Oh, Nicky."

They walked the rest of the way in silence.

When they reached the barn everything was as Nicky had left it earlier. Guinevere was nursing the first foal while the twin lay quietly in the corner. Nicky opened the stall door and went in with Janie close behind him. Guinevere eyed them suspiciously, but the first colt walked right over to them confidently. He stuck his nose out and nuzzled Janie's leg. "Ooh," said Janie, "he's cute."

Nicky knelt down by the foal lying in the corner. He stroked his neck gently. The little ears twitched. How cold he felt, Nicky thought, and he automatically began to massage him, hoping to make the blood flow faster. Janie came and sat beside them. "Can I do anything?" she asked.

"I wish I could think of something else to do," said Nicky. "That's the trouble. There just isn't anything."

"I'll rub when you get tired," she offered.

"Thanks, Janie," said Nicky gratefully.

They were silent for a while, and then the quiet was broken by a change in the foal's breathing. It became labored and irregular. The children looked at each other in horror. "What'll we do?" gasped Janie.

"Call Grandfather quick!" said Nicky. "Run, Janie!"

Janie was off in a flash, and Nicky felt dreadfully alone as he sat helplessly with the foal. He tried raising its head, but that didn't help. At last he put its head on his lap and looked into its face. As he looked, he knew somehow that the baby was dying. The light of life in the foal's eyes was slowly but surely going out. "Don't die!" said Nicky desperately. "Please, please don't die!" But the moment came. He didn't quite know when. He only knew that the little colt left him so quietly that he did not recognize its leavetaking.

When Janie, followed breathlessly by Grandfather, reached the stall, they found him cradling the foal in his arms, hot tears of grief and frustration running down his face unheeded.

3

THE NEXT DAYS were depressing ones in the Davis household. Nicky was so quiet that his mother grew worried about him. But neither she nor anyone else could seem to raise his spirits at all. He never went near the barn except at feed time, and then he rushed through his chores there and left as soon as possible. Soon the Davises found themselves carefully avoiding any mention of ponies, even in general. Grandfather alone refused to follow this line. He talked casually about Guinevere and the surviving foal at every opportunity.

At last, after days of receiving no response from his grandson, he joined him at the barn one evening when Nicky was giving the pony her hay. Grandfather stood silently for a moment or two, watching. Then he said, "How are you coming along with your mare, Nicky? Are you good friends now?"

Nicky looked down at his feet. "I don't know, Grandfather," he muttered.

"Well, how about the colt?" pursued Grandfather. "He's
old enough to put a halter on and start being led. The earlier
the better, you know."

"I don't know how," said Nicky evasively.

"Well, I'll be glad to help you teach him," said Grandfather.

"I have an awful lot of homework," said Nicky. "I don't
think I have time, Grandfather."

"All right, Nicky," said Grandfather evenly. "I think

you'd better get what's bothering you off your chest. Your behavior this past week has left a lot to be desired."

Nicky looked up at him in astonishment and disbelief. "What have I done?" he asked plaintively. "I can't help being unhappy. Don't you understand, Grandfather? I feel so awful about the foal's dying." His eyes filled with tears as he spoke.

"Certainly I understand how the foal's death makes you sad," said Grandfather. "What I don't understand is the way you are coping with your sadness. You won't talk to your family and you neglect your ponies. Tragedy is part of life, Nicky, and what you have experienced is only a tiny piece of tragedy. You'll have to do better, my friend, or when something bigger than this comes along, and it will, you'll find that your shoulders are too puny to bear it."

Nicky looked at his Grandfather indignantly. "I *loved* that foal!" he cried. "And it died right in my arms and I couldn't do anything to save it. I *do* think that's a tragedy."

"Well, I look at it a different way," said Grandfather. "If there's tragedy, it's ahead and it's of your making. You have thrown aside what's left you — a lovely little mare and her fine colt — because you can only think of what's gone. You resent the living, Nicky — you resent the living."

Nicky opened his mouth and stared at him.

"You have forgotten all about a pony that you were thrilled with ten days ago, and the lovely colt she's given you. All because you couldn't play God and save an extra dividend. I know you worked over that foal the short time he lived. If you'll think about it, that's why you favored him. Work over the mare and the foal that are still here and you'll find that they will fill your heart too. We love what we take trouble over."

Nicky sighed. "I'm sorry, Grandfather," he said slowly. "I'll try to be better. Honest I will."

Grandfather smiled. "You haven't even named the foal yet. Why don't we think of a good name for him now?"

"Okay," said Nicky, "only I sort of don't know where to begin."

"Well, let's start by thinking of the parents' names," said Grandfather. "Guinevere and Gawain. King Arthur's court, you know. How about another name from the Round Table?"

"Yes," said Nicky with the ghost of a smile. "That would be nice. Gosh, there was Lancelot and Galahad and Tristram, and oh, lots of them." He was silent for a minute. Then he said, "I know, Grandfather, I just thought of the name that I want him to have. It's part of the legend too, but it's not one of the knights. There were so many of those. Let's call him Merlin after the most famous magician that ever was."

"That's a fine name," said Grandfather. "Merlin it is."

They both automatically turned and looked at the colt. He looked back at them boldly. Nicky felt as if he were really seeing him for the first time. He noted the tiny ears and muzzle and the big eyes. The baby had "a leg on four corners" too. Nothing weak or crooked about him. He was so dark as to appear black, but he had a large star on his forehead and three white socks to catch the attention. Grandfather looked at the fine hairs around Merlin's eyes. "He'll turn," he said. "It'll take a long while but one day he'll be as white as his mother."

Guinevere stamped and nodded her head at a fly, and Nicky laughed. "She agrees with you, Grandfather," he said.

From that evening on, in his spare time Nicky could be found playing with Guinevere and Merlin. The little mare became completely at ease with him and began to depend on him for the affection and care that she had lacked the better part of her life. Merlin, of course, had no unpleasant memories to overcome and was friendly and playful from the beginning. Nicky groomed each of them thoroughly every day, and soon Guinevere's coat shone and glistened like polished marble. Merlin's looked fuzzy because he hadn't shed his baby hair, but it was silky and shiny just the same.

On the days that Janie came over to visit, she was always amazed by the change in the little mare. Guinevere was no longer a wild, unfriendly pony but a gentle and loving companion. One afternoon when the two children were mending a loose board in the fence, Janie asked, "Does Guinevere try to jump these fences, Nicky? I remember your telling me that she was always jumping out of her other owner's pastures."

Nicky laughed. "Nope," he said. "She's never tried it here. Of course, at first she wouldn't have because of Merlin, but now it's because she has enough around home to keep her busy."

As if to prove the truth of this statement, Guinevere, who had been standing beside them lazily switching flies, spied Nicky's shirt, which he had hung on the fence. She glanced at him out of the corner of her eye and then, in a lightning motion, seized the shirt in her teeth and shook it playfully.

"Hey!" cried Nicky. "Drop that! You'll tear it and Mother will skin me alive!"

Guinevere only nodded her head up and down, the shirt flapping wildly. But when Nicky approached her, she dropped it gently at his feet and presented her shoulder to be scratched.

Janie giggled. "She wanted you to pay her some attention, I guess."

"You're right," said Nicky. "She doesn't like to be left out of anything and I suppose she thought you and I had been talking long enough."

Guinevere rested her chin on his shoulder and gazed out across the rolling pastures. There was no longing in her dark eyes at all — only contentment.

4

WHEN SUMMER VACATION CAME, Grandfather said to Nicky, "I think maybe it's about time to start schooling the ponies. Our personal show season is almost here. The Devon spring show is over, of course, but I have Guinevere entered in the National Welsh the end of July. It's being held at Devon also. A show at Devon is quite an experience. It's what you might call the 'big time.' So I've entered her in a smaller show three weeks from Saturday. Actually, there are classes for both the mare and the foal. I think it will be good practice for all three of you."

Nicky asked hesitatingly, "Am I going to show them, Grandfather? I had sort of hoped you would. You know all about it and I don't know anything."

"I'm going to teach you," said Grandfather. "You'll have to start sometime and now's as good a time as any."

So, Nicky worked with Guinevere and Merlin under

Grandfather's direction. He learned how to stand a pony squarely on all four feet so that it appeared to its best advantage. He learned how to keep its attention at all times so that it would not "go to sleep on him" in the ring. "Always remember," said Grandfather, "that who's on the end of a pony's shank may make the difference between a champion and an also-ran. Real showing is hard work, and you can't let up for a second. I've seen many a good showman take a pony to the top that basically had no right to be there. But they were shown to perfection. In the ring their faults were all hidden by their handlers, and a judge can only judge what he sees."

"What are Guinevere's faults, Grandfather?" asked Nicky.

"You're lucky in that she's a pretty top animal," said Grandfather. "However, if I were showing her, I think I would try to get her to stretch her neck a little. It's a mite on the cresty side. If it's stretched it will look finer."

"How about Merlin?" pursued Nicky.

"Well, he's growing in bits and pieces the way most of them do," said Grandfather. "Right now he's grown more behind than in front, so he doesn't look too smooth across the croup. Pinch him gently right over the kidneys. His reaction will be to tighten his muscles there and you will find that he levels out. Soon he will come to anticipate the pinch, and if you run your hand over his back in the ring he will level out for you there."

Nicky put a shank on Merlin and lined him up. Then he pinched where Grandfather had suggested and stood back amazed as the colt immediately leveled his top line. "It works!" he said joyfully.

"Usually does," murmured Grandfather.

"How about Guinevere's neck? How do I make her stretch it?" asked Nicky.

"Always have something in your free hand that interests her," said Grandfather. "Grass, sugar, a piece of cellophane that makes a crinkly noise — all these things work well. But I prefer the cellophane. Otherwise, you could teach her to nip if you're not careful. Here, take this piece from my cigarettes and try it."

Nicky did as he was told. He lined the mare up and then crinkled the cellophane in his hand just beyond her nose. She reached for it, her ears pricked.

"Perfect!" said Grandfather. "But don't make her reach too far or she'll break her stance and move forward."

Nicky's real trouble in the lessons came in moving Guinevere. Try as he would, he could not get her to trot with the lovely reaching stride she had in the pasture. He worried constantly about it, but Grandfather just said, "Keep working, Nicky, it will come. You have to hit just the right stride yourself, too. Otherwise you keep the pony off balance. Practice for you both is the only answer."

"Maybe she'll do it right in the ring, where she's more

excited," panted Nicky after a series of unsuccessful attempts at capturing Guinevere's elusive free trot.

Grandfather frowned. "That's a lazy man's way," he said. "Too many people do their schooling in the ring. It doesn't work out well, believe me. The more you work here, the better your chances there. Keep after it every day, no matter how discouraged you get. It will pay off in the end."

So Nicky kept on. Each afternoon he trotted Guinevere along the paddock fence, hopeful that she would suddenly hit her lovely natural stride. But Guinevere just trotted like any other pony. And then the Thursday before the show it happened. Nicky had turned Guinevere around for her last trot of the afternoon, and as he clucked to her, a horse and rider appeared on the crest of a distant hill. Guinevere's ears pricked and her nostrils widened as she surged forward, and Nicky found himself running as fast as he could to stay even with the trotting pony. Down along the paddock fence they swept, pony and boy in perfect accord. At last Guinevere's brilliance of action was being displayed on the end of a shank. Her tail, raised in excitement, plumed out behind her and shimmered in the late afternoon sun. Nicky's face was full of happiness as he slowed the mare to a walk and patted her. "She did it! Oh, Grandfather, isn't she great?"

Grandfather smiled as the pair approached. "She is in-

deed," he replied. "But if you've got another run in you, try it once more, Nicky, so she'll know that's what you want."

Nicky obediently turned Guinevere again to trot. The horse and rider were gone now, but when Nicky clucked, Guinevere tossed her head and set off again as if she had wings on her heels. When they reached the end of the fence line, Nicky said "Whoa," and she obediently came to a stop with perfect collection and stood still as a statue. Nicky threw his arms around her neck and hugged her. "Guinevere," he whispered, "you're the best pony in all the world."

Guinevere nuzzled him gently as if to say, "So *that's* what you were after all this time. I could have done it in a minute if you had only let me know."

The following day was a full one. The ponies had to be bathed. Janie came over to help. She was going with them the next morning and, as they were leaving very early, Mrs. Davis had invited her to spend the night. She arrived full of excitement just as it was time to wash the ponies. Under Grandfather's direction, the children got them wet all over with warm water and then they soaped them thoroughly with a mild soap. After scrubbing until they were sure the last bit of dirt was gone, they took a wooden scraper and scraped away all the soap.

Then came the rinsing. Grandfather handed them a bucket of warm blue water.

Nicky's eyes widened. "What's that?" he asked.

"That," said Grandfather, "is what a gray pony gets rinsed with. There's bluing in it."

"Won't she turn blue?" asked Janie.

"Are your sheets blue after your mother has washed them?" said Grandfather.

"Well, n–o," said Janie.

"The principle is the same," remarked Grandfather. "Only it's a pony instead of a sheet."

They sponged on the blue water until they could feel no more soap in Guinevere's coat. "What about Merlin?" asked Nicky.

"He's got white socks and a star," said Grandfather. "They will look the better for it too. Actually, I rinsed all my animals with bluing. It can't hurt and generally helps."

So, after both ponies were free of soap and still thoroughly covered with blue water, they were scraped again, and their feet were scrubbed with a stiff brush. Then they were walked in the warm sun until they were dry. How Guinevere glistened! "She looks whiter than the sheets," Janie giggled. "How much bluing did you use, Mr. Stires? I'll have to tell Mother."

Grandfather grinned as he slipped a stable sheet over Guinevere's head. "It's a secret formula," he said.

The children took the ponies back to their stall, which Nicky had cleaned out earlier. They stood now in deep, clean straw, enjoying the attention that was being paid them. Janie carefully combed Merlin's mane and tail, while Nicky performed the same task with Guinevere. "What shall I do to make his mane come over on the right side?" wailed Janie at last, after monumental efforts to achieve this goal. "It just sticks straight up no matter what."

"It's too short still," said Nicky. "It won't fall over till he's older. Don't worry, he looks fine."

Janie stood back and surveyed her handiwork. "He does look cute," she admitted.

The rest of the day was spent in gathering the show tack and cleaning it. Grandfather had produced from the closet in his room a beautiful halter with a name plate on it that said *Elbereth Guinevere*. Nicky gasped when he saw it. "When did you get it, Grandfather?" he asked.

"I saved it," admitted Grandfather. "It's the halter that I had made eleven years ago for this very mare and I never had the heart to part with it. And here's the foal halter that I kept." He handed Nicky another halter, as perfectly made as the first but much smaller, just the right size for Merlin. Then he displayed two lead shanks. "All these things need to be given the once-over," he said. "They are in good shape, to be sure, but a little saddle soap and some brass polish will make them even better. Go to it, kids."

After the job was done, the fine leather gleamed in rich dark splendor and the brass caught the light like gold. The children put the tack carefully in a linen sack with a drawstring. The two red and white brow bands that Nicky had bought under Grandfather's direction were wrapped separately in plastic bags before they were put in with the rest of the tack, lest their patent leather surface be scarred. Then Grandfather dropped two other items into the sack. They were ordinary chain choke collars for dogs — one short one, one long one. Both, however, were made of large rather than fine links.

"What are those for?" asked Janie.

"They go round the ponies' noses and the lead shanks are fastened to them when we show," explained Nicky. "It helps you control your pony better. If you just fasten on to the halter, the pony can really pull you around if it wants to."

When the children fed grain at five, they cleaned the stall of manure, and they did the same thing at hay time after supper. "This way, we hope they stay clean," said Nicky. Nevertheless, they gathered two buckets, one for wash and one for rinse, to take in the morning, together with soap, sponges and bluing. "Just in case," Nicky explained. Before leaving the stable, Grandfather read off the check list of things to be taken.

"Washing equipment."

"Here," said Nicky.

"Grooming equipment."

"Here," said Janie.

"Show tack."

"Here," said both children.

"Manure basket and pitchfork."

"Oops," said Nicky. "Wait a sec." He ran to get them. "Here," he said returning, "but why are we taking them?"

"Aren't you keeping this stall clean?" asked Grandfather.

"Yes," said Nicky.

"Well, no sense not keeping the stall at the show the same way."

"Oh," said Nicky.

"My camp chair," said Grandfather.

"Here," said Nicky.

"Fly spray."

"Here," said Janie.

"Hay net."

"Here," said Nicky. "We stuffed it really full."

"Good," said Grandfather. "Well, I guess that does it. Say goodnight to the ponies and off to bed with you. We're leaving at five A.M."

The children left the barn regretfully and made their way up to the house. "I'll never be able to sleep," said Janie. "Will you?"

"No," Nicky admitted, "I'm too excited."

But even though they lay awake for a long time, sleep finally overcame them.

Mrs. Davis knocked on their doors at four-fifteen the next morning. They scrambled into their clothes and clattered down the stairs to the kitchen, where a substantial breakfast awaited them. Grandfather descended more sedately several minutes later and joined them at the table. In about half an hour they heard the sound of the van as it chugged up the lane. Nicky and Janie ran out on the porch and peered into the darkness.

"Whose van have you got?" asked Janie.

"The Harrises' again," said Nicky. "They aren't using it much this year and told Pop that we could borrow it when we needed it."

"Who's driving?" said Janie.

"A man named Jim that used to work for Grandfather when he had the ponies," said Nicky. "He's a neat guy. You'll like him, Janie."

The van pulled to a stop and Grandfather climbed into the cab to direct Jim to the barn. The children followed behind.

Loading went smoothly and soon they were off. Nicky and Janie rode with the ponies while Grandfather rode up front with Jim. It was a very different trip from the last one they had taken. Guinevere didn't seem nervous at all, and Merlin wandered around inside the van completely unconcerned. The two-hour run passed swiftly and uneventfully.

When they reached the show grounds both ponies pricked up their ears, for the place was filled with neighing.

"Must be a million ponies out there," said Janie.

"Well," said Nicky, "there are lots of performance

classes at this show too. Of course we're just in the halter classes. They start at eight-thirty and Guinevere's in the first one."

The van finally stopped and Jim lowered the ramp. The ponies watched with interest as the children carried the equipment off and set it beside the stall assigned to them. Then, after Grandfather had carefully checked the stall to make sure there were no nails or other sharp objects sticking out of the boards, Guinevere and Merlin were led off the van and into the stall.

Jim smiled as he saw the little gray mare in the daylight when Nicky stripped off her stable sheet. "She certainly is a corker," he said. "You've done a real job there, Nick."

Janie went to the secretary's stand to get the numbers while Nicky set to work grooming Guinevere. He started with the currycomb, then used a fairly stiff brush, then a soft one, and ended by polishing her with a rub rag dipped in fly spray. He used a special brush for her mane and tail. When he was finished, she shone like a marble statue.

Janie returned with the numbers and the show catalogue, which she gave to Grandfather. He flipped through it and then frowned slightly.

"Something wrong, Mr. Stires?" Janie asked.

"Sam Jackson's got his whole string here," he said. "I'd hoped that he wouldn't bother with this show."

Nicky's heart began to thump. Suddenly he was afraid. How could *he* show Guinevere against Mr. Jackson's mares? It wasn't fair to Guinevere. Mr. Jackson had top-notch handlers as well as topnotch animals.

"Grandfather," he whispered, "won't you please show Guinevere?"

"Grandfather looked at him intently. "This is a show for you to learn in, Nicky," he said. "That's why we're here. Actually, when I come to think of it, I'm glad Sam shipped in. Then you'll know your top competition for the National. Don't worry about anything. Keep your mind on your pony and do your best. That's the important thing. If you make mistakes today, you will learn from them."

"Okay," said Nicky with a gulp. He drew a deep breath and started to polish Merlin with the rub rag.

Guinevere looked at him curiously. Her friend seemed nervous. If he was nervous maybe she should be nervous too. She stamped a foot and began to walk the stall.

Just then Grandfather came in with the show tack. "We might as well get ready," he said. After glancing at Nicky he added, "Here, you do Merlin and I'll do Guinevere." Under his sure hands, the mare quieted down. His attitude reassured her that all was well.

When the ponies were ready and Nicky had tied his number around his waist, they left the stall and walked them slowly to ringside. Grandfather scanned the grassy ring. Then he pointed out a spot to Nicky. "We'll try to line up there," he said. "It's level, while the rest of the ring has some bad spots. A pony can't show its best if it has to stand uphill or downhill — even a little bit."

Nicky nodded. His mouth felt too dry to speak. Some of the other exhibitors were approaching now. Soon they would be called into the ring.

Grandfather looked at him understandingly. "All of us, even the best of us, are frightened a little when we first go out in the ring," he said. "But the important thing is to try to forget yourself and just think about your pony, and the way you can do best by her. You are proud of her, so let the judge know it. Don't slink off into a corner with her. When they call the class, you and I are going to enter the ring first and we're going in at a trot. You let Guinevere really trot out, now, all the way around the ring. Don't worry about Merlin and me. We'll keep up."

"Okay," said Nicky.

Grandfather handed Nicky Guinevere's shank and took Merlin's as the ring announcer said over the loudspeaker, "Class I in the ring, please. Welsh broodmares with foals at foot. Class I in the ring, please."

Grandfather grinned at Nicky. "All right, Nicholas," he said, "let's show the folks what a top pony looks like."

Nicky clucked to Guinevere and she responded perfectly. Through the in gate they swept and into the ring at a spanking trot. Guinevere seemed almost to float as she circled the ring. Her hooves, which Nicky had polished with oil, flashed over the grass and her tail plumed out like a banner. Nicky slowed her regretfully to a walk as more ponies began to enter the ring, but not before he had heard the "Ohs" of the crowd that had gathered outside the fence. The judge, who was standing at the center, couldn't seem to take his eyes off the little silver mare who moved so proudly.

The class was filling rapidly now.

"There are fourteen entries which, counting foals, makes twenty-eight animals," said Grandfather to Nicky as they walked along. "This is a small ring. Try not to get yourself boxed in. Guinevere likes to move out, and if she gets caught behind a slowpoke she may fret."

"What do I do if we get behind one?" asked Nicky.

"Look for a bigger space in the line and cut over to it," answered Grandfather. "Actually, as long as the class isn't closed you can move almost anywhere. Once all the entries are in, though, and the judging starts, you have to be careful not to interfere with another pony by getting between it and the judge. Some people do it, of course, but it's a trick that gives you a bad name and rightly so."

At last the gate was closed and the judging began. Nicky found that he was behind a chestnut mare which walked rather slowly and in front of a gray which walked rapidly. In fact she seemed to be walking almost on Guinevere's heels. Nicky began to get nervous. "What'll I do, Grandfather?" he whispered.

Grandfather glanced round the ring quickly. It was a solid line of ponies — not a space to be seen.

"Take it easy," he murmured. "I should have figured this one, but I guess I'm rusty. We're stuck between Sam's two top mares and we're getting a little bit of the business. We'll be asked to line up soon, though."

He was right. The ringmaster asked the exhibitors to bring their ponies in to the center and line up for the judge. Guinevere was fidgeting now and Nicky noted that she was beginning to sweat. Merlin, however, seemed to be having the time of his life. When they had lined up, Nicky still found himself in uncomfortably close quarters. He had moved to the part of the arena that Grandfather had pointed out before the class, but both Jackson mares had moved there too and had sandwiched him again. An older man was handling the chestnut and a boy of eighteen or so had the gray's shank.

Grandfather turned genially to the man. "Hi there, Tom," he said. "Is Mr. Jackson here today?"

"No, Mr. Stires, he couldn't make it," the man replied.

"You certainly have two fine animals in this class," said Grandfather. "But you know, they're a little too close for comfort. Much as I like 'em, I'd like to see them from a bit further off."

The boy with the gray laughed. "It's right crowded, isn't it?" he said. "But then, that's the way it goes in some classes."

Grandfather frowned but said nothing more. Tom gave them a little more room but the boy moved his mare even closer.

"Understand you have something of a wildcat in that pony," he said. "She does look sort of edgy now, doesn't she?"

Unfortunately, he was speaking the truth. Guinevere was sweating profusely by now and she refused to stand still. She sidled and backed and rolled her eyes. Nicky began to get frightened. He could not seem to quiet her. At last the judge reached them and for a moment she stood still. Nicky breathed a sigh of relief. The judge smiled at him and said, "How old is your pony, son?"

"Twelve, sir," replied Nicky. "But she's never been in a

show before," he added quickly. "I guess that's why she's sort of upset."

"Well, I'd like you to move her for me if you will," said the judge. "Please walk down to the end of the ring and trot back."

Nicky did as he was told. Guinevere walked as if she were ready to explode and Nicky wondered what she would do coming back, but she surprised him by trotting beautifully. He started to slow her down to get back in his old place, but Grandfather said in a low tone, "Keep going. Keep going. Get up to the end of the line that has been judged already." So Nicky obeyed.

At the other end of the lineup he found things much easier. No animals crowded him and Guinevere settled down a little.

Finally each pony had been individually judged. The steward then called out the numbers of the ponies that the judge wanted to look at again. Nicky's number was called first. He was asked to line up in a separate line, as were five other ponies. The Jackson mares were included in the group.

"Head to tail, please," said the steward.

Again the boy with the gray was behind them, and though Nicky and Guinevere were at the head of the line and could move forward if necessary, somehow Nicky still felt squeezed. The judge was moving in their direction when the boy with the gray said, "Hey, kid, your pony sure is a worrywart. This old gal I've got — why, *nothing* can shake her. I'd better wake her up. Look at this."

He raised the whip that he held in his free hand and slashed it downward to the ground. It made a whistling sound and then a thwack. And at that moment Guinevere went to pieces. She reared sky-high and then plunged forward, dragging Nicky with her. If it hadn't been for Grandfather, who in a lightning-swift motion grabbed her shank, she would have hurdled the fence that enclosed the ring. As it was, Nicky was slammed up against the rails. Grandfather struggled with Guinevere while Merlin, who by this time was upset too, added to the confusion. The steward ran to help and the judge put his arm around Nicky's shoulder and asked, "Are you all right?" Nicky nodded, fighting back tears. He returned to where Grandfather held Guinevere, who was truly in a terrible state. The sweat was dripping off her belly and she was kicking at it in a distracted way. Her eyes were wild. Grandfather was talking to her gently but firmly, and gradually she grew calmer till she stood fairly quietly, but long shivers of fright ran over her body.

Grandfather's face was grim as he gave Nicky's hand a squeeze. "I'm afraid you've had your baptism of fire, Nicky," he said. "In all my years of showing I've never seen a dirtier trick, and in all the years you have ahead of you, you never will. Do you want to take your pony now? I think it would be the best thing for both of you if

you did. See if you can calm her and give her back her confidence."

Nicky took the shank and spoke softly to Guinevere. He was surprised to find that he was no longer scared, and when she pushed her head into his shoulder as if seeking his protection, he knew that he would never be frightened with Guinevere again. He suddenly realized that she depended on him completely — that he had to be brave and confident enough for both of them. If she felt that he was upset, her sense of security would disappear and she would become as wild as the day he bought her. "Poor Guinevere," he murmured, stroking her lathered neck. "It's all right now. Everything will be all right."

Just then the judge approached them. "I have been talking to the young gentleman with the overactive whip," he said in a serious tone. "He says that he used it only as a strong measure to alert his pony, who is inclined to be rather lackadaisical in the ring. Technically, he is within his rights, but I feel that you are certainly at liberty to make a protest. I'm afraid that I can't pin your lovely little mare because of the temperament problem that she has shown, but I do want you to know that outside of that factor the class was yours, hands down."

"Thank you," said Grandfather slowly. "I think it means a lot to my grandson just now to hear you say that."

The judge smiled. "Better luck with her next time," he said to Nicky. "She is a truly unusual mare."

Nicky said shyly, "Thank you, sir. *I* think she is."

They walked from the ring as the ribbons were awarded. Grandfather turned to Nicky when they reached the stall. "I'm tremendously proud of you," he said. "I don't suppose I'll ever be able to tell you what it means to me — what you did out there."

Nicky blinked at him. "What do you mean?" he asked. "Why, I goofed up the whole thing! I was so scared that Guinevere didn't have anyone to depend on. That's why she got so wild, really. It wasn't the guy with the whip as much as it was me."

"That's just what I mean," said the old man. "I saw you get frightened and then, after the worst that could happen had happened, I saw you overcome your own fear for the sake of your pony. That's why I'm proud of you. Because your love for Guinevere is based on complete understanding and because you showed true courage, which is the defeat of one's own fear."

Nicky looked up at his grandfather and smiled, but before he could say anything, Janie burst upon them, followed closely by Jim. "That guy was horrible!" she cried, her cheeks flushed with anger. "I've never seen a meaner trick in all my life! Can't you do something about it?"

"Yes," said Jim. "Aren't you going to file a protest, Mr. Stires? You have every right to!"

"I don't think so," said Grandfather. "He certainly didn't strike our animal — or even his own, for that matter.

We've all seen ponies waked up a bit by their handlers in that way. The fact that Guinevere minded it was our problem, not his."

"But what about all the crowding?" protested Jim.

"That again could have been accidental and certainly was not an obvious interference with Guinevere," said Grandfather. "Anyway, I think we have our little problem licked, so a protest isn't too important. After all, this class was just practice for us, and it has provided, in its own way, the best possible test. I believe that both Nicky and Guinevere passed it with flying colors!"

Janie and Jim both looked confused, but Nicky said with a grin, "Grandfather's right — because, do you know, I can't wait to get back in there with Merlin."

"Good lad," said Jim, slapping him on the back. "That's the right spirit. You surely take after your granddad."

"How much time is there before Merlin's class?" asked Janie.

"Time enough to rinse Guinevere off and get her dry," said Grandfather.

Janie brought a bucket of warm water and she and Nicky sponged the mare and scraped her until the sweat was gone. Then Nicky walked her dry by taking her all around the show grounds while Janie followed with Merlin. Guinevere was tense and spooky at first, but as she sensed Nicky's calm she began to relax and enjoy the sights and sounds of the show. Soon she was dry and clean once more, the picture pony of an hour before.

When Merlin's class was called, Nicky gave the mare's shank to Grandfather and took the colt's shank himself. Janie tied his new number round his waist and they were off.

The boy with Jackson's gray mare was not in the ring this time. "Must have had a filly at foot," said Grandfather.

There were eight colt foals competing in the class. Consequently, there was considerably more room than before. Everything went perfectly for Nicky. Merlin lined up beautifully and posed for the judge, who walked round him several times. When he was asked to move, he did so willingly, and his trot was a miniature model of his mother's. As they lined up in place once more, Grandfather whispered to Nicky, "That colt is a real ham!" He was

right. Merlin acted as if the show ring were a stage on which to exhibit himself to best advantage. And when the winners were announced, his number was called first. Nicky, full of excitement, trotted him up to get his blue ribbon, and Merlin took the whole thing in his stride. He didn't even object to the rosette fluttering from his halter, although most of the other exhibitors carried theirs out instead of putting them on the foals.

When they arrived back at the stall, Janie was jumping up and down. "You did it!" she squealed. "You did it! Oh, this is wonderful!"

"You know the ribbon is partly yours, Janie," said Grandfather. "After all, you helped get Merlin ready, and condition like his counts for an awful lot."

Nicky nodded his agreement and Janie grinned from ear to ear. "Well, it's fun to help," she said.

"Now," said Grandfather, "since this show has no Junior Championship Class, I guess we're all through. So let's load up and start home. It's been an interesting morning and I think we need to discuss it all at home over cookies and some of your mother's cool lemonade."

During the ride home, Nicky explained to Janie what had happened to Guinevere in the ring. "You see," he said, "the next time I show her, I mustn't get frightened myself or she will get frightened too, and something that ordinarily wouldn't bother her much will scare her to death — like the sound of that whip."

"But still," said Janie stubbornly, "it was a dirty trick."

When they reached home, they unloaded everything and then turned Guinevere and Merlin into the pasture so they could get the kinks out and relax. Janie watched in dismay as first one and then the other picked out the only muddy spot in the entire field for a good roll. "Look at them!" she wailed. "All that work, and now look at them!"

Grandfather laughed. "All they know is that it feels good," he said. "They don't worry about getting clean again. They figure you kids can take care of that."

"And they're right," said Nicky.

At that moment Mrs. Davis called from the porch, "Aren't you pony people ever going to come up and have a little refreshment?"

"Well, Jim," said Grandfather, "how about some lemonade?"

"Sounds good to me, Mr. Stires," said Jim.

So they all went up to the house. Nicky gave Merlin's blue ribbon to his mother. She looked at it, delighted. "How wonderful!" she exclaimed. "Did Guinevere — "

"No," said Grandfather. "That's Merlin's. But the one who deserves a ribbon most of all is a two-legged boy."

And he proceeded to tell the whole story from beginning to end. When he finished, Mrs. Davis looked at Nicky with a smile. "What a good job, Nicky," she said. "And how proud of you I am. But Father," she added, turning to Grandfather, "I'm awfully surprised that Sam

Jackson should have someone like that showing his ponies. He's such an honest man and so are the people who work for him."

Then Jim spoke up. "I did a little scouting at the show, Mrs. Davis," he said. "And I found out that Mr. Jackson just hired the boy — Joe Simpson's his name — a few weeks ago. Mr. Jackson wasn't there today, but you can bet your bottom dollar if he had been, Simpson would have been out of a job."

"I'm sure that's true, Amanda," said Grandfather. "Jim told me that from what he had found out, Simpson came to Sam highly recommended, but Sam had never seen him work in the ring."

"But what about the National?" asked Janie. "He can do the same thing there."

"Ah, but it won't work," said Grandfather with a smile. "Nicky and Guinevere will be ready for anything in the National."

"Gee, Grandfather," said Nicky, "I know what went wrong today, but I sure would like to take Guinevere in the ring again before we go to Devon, just so we can both get used to it."

"That's just what you are going to do," said Grandfather. "If I am right, there are one or two local shows with Junior Showmanship Classes in them. We can enter you and Guinevere. It will be very good for you both."

5

AND SO NICKY AND GUINEVERE, accompanied by Grandfather, Janie, Jim and Merlin, attended two extra shows. They had a great deal of fun. Nicky won two ribbons — a third and a fourth, but most important of all, he won his battle with himself. He learned to think only of his pony and to forget his own nervousness. Guinevere responded to his manner and was calm and under control at all times.

One important decision, however, was reached as a result of the extra shows. It was agreed upon not to show Merlin in the foal class at Devon, since he was becoming a little growthy to be the perfect picture foal. "He's reached the awkward age," said Grandfather with a smile. "To be completely fair to him, we shouldn't show him for a while. A pony should never be shown unless he's at his best. But wait till next year!"

The day of departure for Devon finally arrived. Grandfather had decided to ship in the night before the show, so that the ponies would feel rested and at home in their new surroundings by class time. So, besides washing the ponies and gathering together all the equipment they had taken before, Nicky and Janie assembled some extra things to go on the van. Grandfather had made up a new list. He read it off. It included four sleeping bags, a folding table and four chairs, a Thermos, a box of paper cups, grain enough for two meals, feed and water buckets, extra hay and straw, colic medicine, a dose syringe, and a bottle of gentian violet, called "blue" by horsemen.

These last three items, Grandfather collected himself. "This way, if a pony gets hurt or has colic, we can do something about it while we wait for the vet."

It was midafternoon when Mr. and Mrs. Davis waved good-by as the van rolled down the lane. "Grandfather says we'll be all ready to relax by suppertime," said Nicky to Janie, as they settled down comfortably on the extra bales of straw.

"This is really exciting," said Janie. "I've never been at a show grounds overnight before."

"Me neither," said Nicky. "We have a tack stall next to the ponies and we'll sleep there in the sleeping bags. It will be just like camping out!"

The trip passed quickly, and before they knew it they were at the Devon Show Grounds. Nicky and Janie, peeping out the windows of the van, both gasped as they pulled in the entrance. "Gee, it's beautiful!" said Janie.

"It sure is," agreed Nicky. "Look at the grandstand and ring! And how about that stabling? That's really neat!"

It was a lovely sight. Set among old trees, the ring shone emerald-green, flanked by its fresh white grandstand. Past the grandstand and wandering off among the trees was a walkway lined by charming pavilions. Ponies were schooling in a practice ring and over an outside jumping course. The whole atmosphere was one of anticipation and friendly competition. Everyone seemed to know everyone else, and as people passed, their conversation drifted up to the children.

From two men walking side by side: "Have you brought your good little chestnut stud that I saw at Upperville?"

"Yes, he's here, but we got beat by Sam's gray last time out. I'm afraid he's a bit too much for us."

Or from a group of three, leading ponies in driving harness: "The trip wasn't too bad. But it's good to be here and settled in. Monarch threw a shoe this morning and I was fit to be tied. I didn't know you Easterners knew how to shoe a harness pony like we do back home."

"Oh come on, Dick — we have a few good harness ponies here too, you know. We don't specialize in hunting types entirely."

"Well, I have to say the blacksmith did a darn fine job. Must have come from my part of the country."

They all laughed at that and then passed out of earshot. The van pulled to a stop before a neat low barn and

[83]

Grandfather poked his head in the door. "Are you two ready to unload?" he asked.

"Yes, sir," replied Nicky. The ramp was lowered and the children and Jim carried the equipment to one of the two beautiful stalls they found waiting for them. Then, after checking out the ponies' stall and putting bedding down, they unloaded Guinevere and Merlin and brought them to their new quarters. Both ponies seemed quite at ease, though Guinevere rubbed her head on Nicky's shoulder at first for reassurance. He showed her her water bucket and feed tub and then led her to the forkful of hay that he had put in the stall. She sniffed it, heaved a sigh, and took a wisp or two. He patted her gently and soon she was eating contentedly while Merlin, who felt that this was no time for eating, explored the stall and pricked his ears at the voices of strange ponies. He was having a fine time.

Meanwhile, Grandfather directed Jim and Janie in the sleeping arrangements next door. The sleeping bags were lined up against the walls. The tack bag, grooming box and medicine kit were under the table, which was set up in the middle of the stall with the four chairs around it. Soon all was shipshape, and Grandfather said, "Well, I guess that does it. Jim, you'd better move the van to the parking area. And Janie, if I give you a dollar or two, do you think you could scare us up something cool to drink and maybe something to eat along with it? Just a snack, now. I don't want to spoil appetites for supper."

"You bet, Mr. Stires!" said Janie. She took the money

and was off like a flash. Grandfather came over to the ponies' stall and looked in. "How's everything, Nicky?" he asked. "Is she settling in all right?"

"Yes, she's fine, Grandfather," said Nicky.

"Good," said Grandfather. He looked at his watch. "I guess we might as well feed up, then."

He pulled out the bag of feed, measured some into a bucket and handed it to Nicky, who poured it into Guinevere's feed tub. She came over at once and began to eat, while Merlin shouldered his way between his mother and Nicky so that he could share the grain.

Then Grandfather measured out the feed for Merlin and Nicky put that in a bucket in another corner of the stall. He led the reluctant colt back to his own dinner and tied him there. Then he tied Guinevere too, so that if she finished first she wouldn't steal her son's meal.

"We won't have any trouble weaning him as far as his eating is concerned," laughed Grandfather as Merlin buried his nose in the bucket.

"No," agreed Nicky. "He loves his grain. He's cleaning up four quarts a day now and I guess I'll have to increase him pretty soon."

Just then Janie came back carrying Cokes and cookies.

"Here you are, Mr. Stires," she announced, setting them on the table, "and here's your change."

"Oh, I think you've earned that change," said Grandfather. "This looks very tempting."

"Gee, thanks," said Janie with a grin.

Jim arrived, and they all sat down around the table and had a very pleasant snack. When the Cokes were gone and the cookies were eaten, Grandfather said, "Now, kids, Jim and I will be relaxing here for a while, so why don't you take a look around the show grounds? But be back in an hour, okay?"

"Okay!" said Nicky and Janie.

They scampered off down the long aisle of the barn. On either side were the roomy box stalls, some housing sleek ponies, some set up as tack rooms. Most of the tack rooms were very elaborate, draped with cloth from ceiling to floor so that the stall seemed like a roomy tent. This cloth could even be dropped completely over the door to insure privacy, but was generally drawn back to display the inside of the stall, where ribbons and pictures of the ribbon winners hung on the walls. Janie and Nicky stopped before a tack room that was truly magnificent. Its cloth, like that of the other tack rooms, was dyed in the owner's colors. This one was crimson edged with midnight blue. The word *Pemberton* was emblazoned in blue across one side.

"Hey, Janie," Nicky whispered. "That's Mr. Jackson's stable."

They moved closer and looked in. Lined neatly along the walls were tack trunks, also in the stable colors. Scores of ribbons hung against the cloth backdrop. Many were the tricolors of championships. Under them were pictures

of their winners, complete with neatly written pedigrees and show records. A four-pronged bridle hook was suspended from the ceiling and a man was cleaning one of the beautiful show bridles that hung from it. In the corner of the room was a rocking chair, and in the rocking chair was Mr. Sam Jackson. He looked up at the children and smiled. "Hello there, kids," he said. "Would you like to come in?"

Nicky and Janie looked at each other. Then Nicky said shyly, "Yes, sir."

They stepped gingerly into the room. Mr. Jackson motioned genially to some chairs. "Sit down," he said, "and make yourself comfortable. Is this your first visit to the National?"

They nodded. Mr. Jackson looked at Nicky curiously and asked, "Haven't I met you somewhere, son? I'm pretty good about remembering faces but I'm not much on names."

"Yes, sir," said Nicky. "It was at Timonium in May. Grandfather and I bought a pony that you were bidding on too."

"Now I remember," said Mr. Jackson. "You're David Stires's grandson. Well, how's your little mare? Did she have a nice filly for you?"

"No, it was a colt, but a real good one," said Nicky. "Actually, it was twins. We lost the other colt," he added sadly.

"That was tough luck," said Mr. Jackson kindly. "But

she'll have lots of fine foals for you, I know. Have you bred her back?"

"Not yet," said Nicky.

"Well, then," said Mr. Jackson, "I have a selling job to do. How do you like my stud?"

"I've never seen him," said Nicky truthfully.

Mr. Jackson waved at a picture on the wall. "That's him," he said. "The ribbons are this year's crop."

Nicky looked at the picture and said, "He looks very nice, sir."

Mr. Jackson grinned. "You sound as if David had educated you a bit," he said. "You're perfectly right. A man ought always to see what he's breeding his mare to in the flesh."

Nicky grinned sheepishly. "Grandfather did tell me that," he admitted.

"And he was correct. Oh, Tom," said Mr. Jackson.

"Yes, sir," said the man who was cleaning the bridle, and whom Nicky recognized as the man who had shown the chestnut mare.

"I would like to show Starfire to this young man. Would you bring him out and move him a bit for us, please."

"Sure thing, Mr. Jackson," said Tom. He left the tack room and Mr. Jackson rose from his chair and walked to the door.

"Come on, children," he said. "I want you to see what I consider to be a topnotch Welsh stallion."

Nicky and Janie joined him. They heard a commanding neigh, and then out of a stall and down the aisle pranced a magnificent gray pony. Although he seemed full of fire and excitement, he did not fight the shank that Tom held but almost danced his way towards them, his neck arched and his eyes glowing. At last he stood before them, still as a statue, but majestic even in repose.

Nicky drew in his breath sharply. Just as Guinevere seemed feminine perfection to him, so did this stallion seem her counterpart in masculine beauty.

"Walk around him," said Mr. Jackson. "Check him out for yourself."

Nicky did so almost in a trance. He could find no fault in the stud at all. Then he remembered Grandfather's teaching. "Would you mind moving him for me?" he almost whispered, feeling very silly indeed.

Mr. Jackson laughed. "I see you're one to be reckoned with. Move him out for us, Tom."

And so Starfire was first walked and then trotted up and down the aisle several times. He moved gaily and yet with tremendous power, as straight and true as an arrow.

"Well," said Mr. Jackson as Tom returned the stud to his stall, "what do you think of him?"

"He's beautiful!" breathed Nicky. Janie nodded in enthusiastic agreement.

"Well, then, why don't you book your little mare to him?" suggested Mr. Jackson. "To tell you the truth, I'd love to see the result of that breeding. I think it ought to be something special."

Nicky looked up at Mr. Jackson with a big smile. "I think that would be fine, sir," he said.

"Good," said Mr. Jackson. "I'll see if we can't work out a reduced fee. Starfire stands at a pretty high figure, but I think in this case it could be lowered."

"Oh no, Mr. Jackson," said Nicky. "I wouldn't want you to do that. Anyway, isn't that part of the bet?"

"The bet?" asked Mr. Jackson, puzzled.

"Yes," said Nicky. "I mean the bet you and Grandfather had. About Guinevere being champion mare?"

Mr. Jackson stared at him. "You mean that David really was serious?" he said incredulously. "You're showing tomorrow?"

"Yes, sir," said Nicky. "And I'm so glad I've seen Starfire because it'll make me work even harder in the ring. If I start to get scared, I'll just remember him and the bet."

Mr. Jackson shook his head disbelievingly. "Have you seen my gray mare Morgana?" he asked.

"I'm not sure," admitted Nicky.

"Well, come along here for a minute," said Mr. Jackson. He led them to a stall which held the gray mare that had shown against them before. "She hasn't been defeated this year," said Mr. Jackson.

Nicky looked carefully at the pony. She was lovely, but somehow to him she lacked the X quality that Starfire and Guinevere had — the quality that attracted attention immediately and held it. "It's almost as if she didn't like any of this," he thought. "She does it because she's asked to, but she'd rather not."

"She *is* pretty, Mr. Jackson," he said, "but I'd still like to win Grandfather's bet for him."

Mr. Jackson laughed ruefully. "Well, well," he said, "I hope you're not too downhearted after tomorrow. Is your grandfather here?"

"Oh yes," said Nicky. "We're up at the other end of the

barn. Janie and I are on leave — sort of. I know he'd like to see you," he added. "Shall I go back and tell him where you are?"

"No indeed," replied Mr. Jackson. "I'll go on up there myself and pay a visit. Besides, maybe I'd better look over my competition. You all run along now and have some fun. I'll see you later, I imagine."

"Thank you so much for showing us Starfire and inviting us into the tack room," said Nicky.

"Not at all, I enjoyed it," said Mr. Jackson briskly. He turned and headed towards the far end of the barn.

Nicky and Janie roamed through the barns and over the grounds in a state of constant excitement. Everywhere they went they saw things that were new to them. Unused to the harness ponies, they marveled at their brilliant action and sleek lines. Then they watched a trotting pony make its workout. It sped over the ground as fast as a galloping pony, but it never broke its trot. The driver called encouragement. It flicked an ear and turned on an extra burst of speed that left the children dazzled. "They have lots of pony racing now," said Nicky to Janie. "Just like the trotting races for horses. But I've never seen a trotting pony before."

"Me neither," said Janie.

They watched hunting ponies schooling over fences, jumping cleanly and alertly.

Then they saw some of the B Welsh — ponies which ex-

ceeded the height limit of 50 inches for the A division. Many of these were fitted as hunters. They were very handsome indeed.

"And all of these are registered Welsh?" asked Janie incredulously at last.

"Yes," said Nicky. "Now you can see why Welsh are such terrific ponies. They're tops at everything." Then he glanced at his watch. "Gee, Janie, we're late!" he said. "For Pete's sake, let's hurry!"

They turned and ran for their barn as fast as they could. As they reached Guinevere's stall they slowed down. After a quick look at his mare, Nicky peeped over the door of the tack stall. Grandfather and Jim and Mr. Jackson were sitting around the table. They were laughing at something Mr. Jackson had said. They looked up as the children entered.

"Just on time," said Grandfather.

"No, I'm afraid we're a little late," said Janie timidly.

"Not at all," said Grandfather. "I tacked on an extra fifteen minutes because I knew you all would get interested and forget."

"Oh," said both children, embarrassed.

"Did you see a lot of ponies?" asked Mr. Jackson.

"Yes!" said Nicky. "And doing such a lot of different jobs!"

"That's why I'm so proud of our breed," said Grandfather. "You can ask a Welsh to do just about anything and he'll do it. And do it well."

"I guess I'd better be running along," said Mr. Jackson. "And I'm going to remember to tell Joe Simpson that he's going to have more competition than he counted on tomorrow. He'll have to keep Morgana on her toes."

"I imagine he will. He's a sharp boy in the ring," said Grandfather.

Mr. Jackson looked at Grandfather. "What do you mean, David?" he asked. "Have you seen him show?"

"We showed against him," said Grandfather quietly.

"How did you do?" asked Mr. Jackson.

"We were disqualified because our mare went to pieces in the ring," said Grandfather.

Mr. Jackson frowned. "That's interesting," he said. "Very interesting. And Morgana won. Well, well." He turned to Nicky. "I'll be at ringside tomorrow and I almost think I'll be rooting for you, Nicky," he said. "I'm very much impressed with your little mare." And he stumped out of the stall and down the aisle.

"Why didn't you tell him what really happened, Mr. Stires?" asked Janie.

"Sam's a wily old bird," said Grandfather. "He can put two and two together. Besides, I don't want to give the boy a bad name for one offense. Let's see how it goes tomorrow."

He reached under the table and pulled out a basket.

"Your mother has fixed us a very fancy dinner," he said to Nicky. "Why don't you feed hay and check the water bucket while Janie and Jim and I get this all arranged?"

Nicky filled the net with hay and went into the ponies' stall. Guinevere nickered to him in greeting. He hung the net where both she and Merlin could reach it. Then, after patting them both and making sure that the water bucket was full, he returned to the tack stall.

He found his place at the table set with a paper plate full of cold fried chicken. By the plate was a cupful of iced tea from the Thermos, and in the middle of the table sat a beautiful cake with strawberry icing.

"Oh boy!" said Nicky.

"And there's a watermelon in the basket, too," said Janie, her mouth full of chicken.

They had a wonderful meal, and after all was put away Grandfather said, "I guess we're in order now and can relax. Kids, you have about an hour before bedtime. What would you like to do?"

Nicky and Janie looked at each other. Then Janie said, "Could you tell us about some of the showing you did, Mr. Stires? You know — about the ponies that were showing then and the people who owned them?"

Grandfather looked pleased. "Well," he began, "I've seen a lot of old familiar faces today, but a lot of new ones too. Seems the biggest difference between then and now is the number of owners. The Welsh pony has sold himself to the public. It looks as if he's really come into his own."

He went on to tell the children about his experiences in the ring, describing the top ponies of his day and occasionally calling on Jim to supply extra information. His tale was often interrupted, however, since friends were continually dropping in and, after being introduced all around, staying awhile to talk old times.

Soon the hour was up. Nicky and Janie checked the ponies to make sure they were comfortable, and then crawled into their sleeping bags. Grandfather turned off the overhead light and they lay in semi-darkness, listening to the sounds of a show grounds at night. They heard occasional whinnies, the noise of vans pulling in, people's voices, low in conversation or calling to each other, but through it all the friendly sound of ponies munching hay. This was the pleasant familiar noise that lulled the children to sleep at last.

6

NICKY AWOKE EARLY the next morning. He climbed out of his sleeping bag and looked around the stall. Janie was still asleep. Grandfather and Jim sat at the table having a cup of coffee. They both smiled at him. "Have a good night?" asked Grandfather.

"Oh yes," said Nicky. "I didn't wake up once."

"Your ponies had a good night too," said Jim. "They're eating breakfast now."

"Gee, you should have waked me," said Nicky. "They're my responsibility. I'm sorry."

"You've got a job to do today," said Grandfather. "And it was important for you to get as much sleep as you could. How about some breakfast?"

Janie rolled over and looked up at them sleepily. "Did somebody say 'breakfast'?" she asked.

Jim laughed. "They did," he said.

Janie untangled herself from her sleeping bag and joined them at the table. They had honey doughnuts and hot chocolate, both of which tasted very good.

"Now," said Grandfather when they had finished, "we have about an hour till Guinevere's class. Janie, why don't you start grooming her while Nicky changes into his show clothes? That way we won't lose any time."

Nicky took his clean pants, shirt and shoes out of Grandfather's suitcase. He changed into them quickly and put on his tie. Then he wet his comb and slicked down his hair. "You look fine," said Grandfather approvingly.

Nicky went to see how Janie was getting on. He found all was going well. She was putting the last-minute touches on Guinevere.

"Do you need me?" he asked.

"No," said Janie. "You'll only get yourself dirty."

"She's not supposed to be dirty," said Nicky. "Did she get dirty overnight?"

"No," said Janie, "but *boys* always get dirty when they work on something. Just stand still and concentrate on keeping clean."

"Oh, for Pete's sake!" muttered Nicky. In the tack stall, Grandfather chuckled.

As Janie finished with the fly spray, Guinevere's class was called. Janie opened the door and handed Nicky the shank. Grandfather took Merlin's and they were off. They joined the parade of ponies to the ring. Guinevere walked alertly, while Merlin danced his way along.

Outside the ring, Grandfather handed Nicky his number. "Nicky," he said, as the boy tied on number 125, "Guinevere is perfectly at ease. So just go on in and show your pony. Don't worry about a thing. I'll keep an eye peeled for tricks."

Nicky nodded solemnly. "Okay, Grandfather," he said. "I'll sure do my best."

"Nicky," said Janie, "take off your shoe a minute."

"What?" said Nicky, astonished. But Janie had his shoe unlaced and off before he could protest.

"What *are* you doing?" he said frantically. "We're supposed to be in the ring right now!"

"It's a four-leaf clover," said Janie. "I've put it in your shoe for good luck. There," she added as she tied the laces. "Now go in and beat that nasty Joe Simpson for me."

"Well, Nicky, you have your orders," laughed Grand-father. "Let's go."

Nicky clucked to Guinevere and they entered the ring at a trot. There was room to continue at that gait for a good part of the oval, as the class was still filling. Nicky heard whispers when he passed the crowd lining the fence. Guinevere had at least caught the attention of the spectators. It seemed she captured the judge's eye too. He watched her closely for a good while before turning his gaze to another entry. More and more mares entered the ring and Grandfather said, "There should be twenty-five in here according to the program — but I only make it twenty-four."

"Morgana isn't here yet," said Nicky.

No sooner had he spoken than there was a flurry at the in gate and Joe Simpson trotted Mr. Jackson's gray into the ring. He almost ran one pony down as he made his bid for the judge's attention. He took Morgana to the inside of the line of walking ponies and then proceeded to trot her the full length of the arena.

"Showboat," muttered Nicky.

"Hm," was all Grandfather would say.

When the time came to line up, Grandfather said, "Line up behind Morgana if you can, Nicky."

Nicky hastened to obey, but as he fell in line behind the Jackson mare he whispered, "Why?"

"Because Simpson's going to be near us one way or the

other, and I'd rather have him in front," Grandfather whispered back.

Evidently this move was not to Joe Simpson's liking. He slowed Morgana down and looked back, but he had lost his chance to follow Guinevere. There were several ponies in back of her by now. He grinned at Nicky. "You're learning, kid," he drawled, "but I wonder if your pony is."

Nicky made no reply. He was concentrating on lining Guinevere up. She obeyed him willingly and stood poised, watching the other ponies as they took their places. There were two lines of ponies now because there were so many. Nicky, luckily, was in the one which the judge picked to look at first. When the judge reached him, Nicky stood back the length of the shank. He put his hand in his pocket and crinkled some cellophane. Guinevere's ears pricked and she stretched her neck, but still held her stance. The judge walked round them several times. Then he smiled and asked Nicky to walk away from him and trot back.

Grandfather said as they walked off, "Keep going until he tells you to stop. That way you have a nice long way to trot back. And trot on past him and around back into your place."

Nicky obeyed. When he asked Guinevere to trot she fairly flew over the ground. He could hardly keep up with her. When he was lined up behind Morgana once more, he almost welcomed the look of irritation on Joe Simpson's face. It meant that he had done well.

When the numbers of the ponies that the judge had selected were called, his was first, and Morgana's second. Reluctantly, Nicky moved Guinevere to head up a third line. Now Joe would be behind him. However, Grandfather, instead of standing Merlin beside his mother, kept him between Morgana and Guinevere. Though Joe was gesturing a great deal with his whip, it meant nothing to

Merlin, who couldn't be bothered with such things. The judge stood before Guinevere now, and suddenly a whip cracked sharply. Guinevere's eyes widened and she snorted loudly, but just at that moment Grandfather trotted Merlin to a spot somewhat in front of her, and her attention was caught by her foal. She stood still, her eyes and nostrils still huge and her neck and tail arched. Grandfather had turned Joe Simpson's trick into a lucky break.

The judge eyed Guinevere carefully and passed on down the line. He asked several of the handlers to move their ponies, and then he marked his card. Nicky was in the depths of depression. "We're out of it," he thought. "He didn't move us twice."

But when the winners were announced, number 125 was on top. Nicky was so excited he could hardly talk when he left the ring with Guinevere. Janie and Jim ran up full of congratulations, but he just stood and smiled happily. Grandfather also wore a big grin. "Well," he said at last, "I guess our first objective has been reached."

Nicky nodded gleefully.

"Here," said Janie, "the wind has messed her mane up. I'd better start grooming again." So she produced a mane comb from her pocket and a rub rag from under her arm and went to work. When the championship class was called, Guinevere was more shiny than ever.

"Now," said Grandfather, "when we go in this one, trot her in and all the way around, because like as not, that's the only time the judge will see her move. They often judge championships on conformation only, unless it's awfully close."

So Nicky trotted Guinevere the entire oval. At last he pulled her to a walk, as he was all out of breath. "I bet she'd make a good trotting pony," he gasped to Grandfather, who had finally caught up with him.

Grandfather smiled. "I think you're right," he said.

Nicky and Guinevere lined up beside the mare which had won the barren mare class. His heart sank a bit as he looked at her. She was obviously much younger than Guinevere and very stylish indeed. Her handler smiled at him and said, "Congratulations on your win. I watched your class and there was some pretty tough competition."

"Thank you," said Nicky. "You certainly have a pretty mare."

"She's nice, all right," the man admitted. "And she's done awfully well this year."

The judge moved over and studied both ponies carefully. He went from back to front, comparing one against the other. Then he asked that they be lined up head to tail so that he could see both in profile simultaneously. After much deliberation he walked back to the secretary's booth and handed in his card. The loudspeaker crackled. "Class forty-one — Broodmare Champion and Reserve. The winner and Champion Mare of the National Welsh Pony Show is number one-twenty-five, Elbereth Guinevere, owned by Nicky Davis of Parkton, Maryland. Reserve is number eighty-four, Greenwillow's Susan, owned by Greenwillow Farm, Danville, Ohio."

Nicky stood stock still as the applause rang out from the stands and ringside. Grandfather prodded him. "Go on up and get your trophy," he said. "They're waiting for you."

So Nicky trotted Guinevere up to the head of the ring and accepted a lovely trophy and the red, yellow and blue championship ribbon from a very pretty lady. "Congratulations," she smiled, "that's a beautiful pony. Is she yours?"

"Yes," said Nicky with a gulp. "And I'm so very proud of her."

When he met Grandfather at the gate, his eyes were misty. "Just think!" he said. "Champion Guinevere! Doesn't that sound wonderful?"

"It certainly does," said Grandfather, his wrinkled face beaming. "It certainly does."

Mr. Jackson was at the stall when they returned. He shook Grandfather's hand and patted Nicky on the back. "Well, sir," he said, "you've won your bet. And what a win! Congratulations to you both. Starfire will be honored to serve the National Champion Mare. I've got to run now. His class will be going in soon. I can't wish you any more luck, though. I'll have to save it all for myself." And he hurried off.

"What did he mean by that?" asked Janie.

"Well, Starfire is pretty sure to win his division," said

Grandfather. "And then he'll have to go in against Guinevere for the Cymru Cup."

"What's that?" asked Janie.

"It's the cup that the Welsh Pony and Cob Society of America gives each year for the Grand Champion Pony of the show," said Grandfather. "All the champions and reserves are eligible."

"Good grief," said Nicky slowly. "You mean Guinevere has to show against Starfire?"

"Yes," said Grandfather. "That's just what I mean."

"Oh no!" groaned Nicky. "We haven't got a chance!"

"Don't be too sure," said Jim. "I've seen a mare go Grand Champion a number of times."

"That's right, Nicky," said Grandfather. "Don't knock your pony. She's tops and you should never count her out. If you do, you're being unfair to her. Now relax for a while, because there are a good number of classes before the big one."

He sat down on one of the chairs and put a handkerchief over his face. Nicky looked at Janie. "I guess we'd better groom her again," he said.

"Not you," said Janie, "me. Here, have some iced tea. Jim and I got lunch while you were talking to Mr. Jackson. There's a hamburger and some potato chips on the table."

Nicky sat down at the table thoughtfully and began to eat in a halfhearted sort of way. He had seen the Junior Champion colt and filly and was not too worried about

them. But Starfire! Well, he would just have to do the best he could. Guinevere was every bit as good a mare as Starfire was a stallion, he thought with pride; the only trouble was that stallions had so much extra presence and natural flair.

The time came at last. Nicky took Guinevere's shank once more and Grandfather came out from under his handkerchief. They walked slowly to the ring. Then Grandfather stopped and said, "Merlin and I will wait for you here. Good luck, Nicholas."

Nicky looked at him aghast. "But why?" he faltered.

"I'm playing a hunch," said Grandfather. "You're on your own now with a champion mare on the end of your shank. Go on out and do her proud!"

Nicky straightened his shoulders and entered the ring. Halfway around he realized why Grandfather had stayed behind. Guinevere, though she trusted Nicky completely, was a little worried about her foal. She had never moved with such brilliance. Her gaze swept the ring as she pranced around it. She was searching for Merlin.

Nicky lined up beside Starfire and cast a quick look at him. He stood, master of all he surveyed, and was, it seemed to Nicky, the perfect Welsh pony. Then Nicky turned his attention to his own mare. As the judge approached, Merlin nickered from his place at the rail. Guinevere threw up her head. She seemed ready to explode at any second, but Nicky's quiet voice kept her under control. She was a very exciting picture indeed.

It became evident at once that the two senior champions were the class. Time and again the judge surveyed them from every possible angle. Nicky began to worry about Guinevere. She had been standing so long that she was becoming very impatient. He gave a sigh of relief when the judge asked that each pony trot the length of the ring. Starfire went first. He sparkled at a trot. He seemed all power and beauty. His performance was a hard one to follow. However, when Guinevere's turn came, she trotted as if it were the only thing in life worth doing. She almost seemed to float as she breezed over the turf.

It was done. The judge had made up his mind. He turned in his card. "Whatever happens, Guinevere," said Nicky, "I'll never forget this class. To me, you're the best — the very best. And that's the only thing that matters."

The spectators all were silent, waiting for the announcement. And then it came. "Class forty-nine — Grand Champion and Reserve of the National Welsh Show. The Grand Champion and winner of the Cymru Perpetual Championship Cup is — number one-twenty-five, Elbereth Guinevere."

A cheer went up from the crowd.

"Reserve is number forty-seven, Pemberton Starfire."

Guinevere, who had been standing restlessly in the center of the ring, started forward automatically, and Nicky, who was completely stunned and openmouthed, was almost thrown off balance. The crowd laughed sympathetically and Nicky laughed too. Guinevere had logically determined from the day's activities that when the announcer spoke it was time for her to go get a ribbon.

Nicky accepted the beautiful cup, his eyes aglow, and when the Grand Champion's rosette was pinned to Guinevere's halter, he obligingly posed her for pictures.

Suddenly there was a great commotion at the in gate and then two figures flew into the ring. The first was four-legged. It was Merlin, galloping gaily, his lead shank flapping behind him. The second was two-legged — Janie — who was frantically trying to catch him. They arrived almost together. Merlin slid to a stop and kissed his mother, who nuzzled him in return. Janie didn't kiss anybody. She was embarrassed and almost in tears. "He got away from me!" she panted. "I'm so sorry, Nicky, honest I am!" But the crowd and the photographers loved it. At last, when Janie had gotten hold of Merlin again, they walked from the ring, with the applause still sounding in their ears. Nicky tried to reassure Janie that what had happened didn't matter a bit. "Poor Merlin," he said, "I don't blame him. That was a long time to be away from his mother."

"I know," said Janie. "But I shouldn't have let him get loose."

"Forget it," laughed Nicky. "I think it was funny."

"Okay," said Janie with the beginning of a smile. The smile grew and grew until it became a laugh. "I guess it was funny. Merlin tearing around the ring with dumb me after him." She started to giggle uncontrollably. Nicky followed suit, and when Grandfather met them they were both laughing uproariously.

"I don't see anything very funny about the Cymru Cup," he said with a twinkle in his eye.

"There isn't anything funny about *that*," said Nicky, becoming sober immediately. "*That* is just great! It was Janie and Merlin dashing all over that was funny."

"Oh," said Grandfather. "I see. Well, let's put the Grand Champion and her proud son to bed for a while until we can digest what has happened. And then I think you have a rather important telephone call to make."

Nicky stopped short. "Mother!" he cried. "I can't wait to tell her."

At the stall they found many well-wishers waiting for them. Among them was Mr. Jackson. He greeted them with a big smile and said, "Well, David, I'm not a man that likes to lose, but if I have to lose, it's nice to be beaten by as fine a pony as Guinevere. There's only one thing that's eating me."

"What's that?" asked Grandfather.

"That I didn't up you another fifty at Timonium," said Mr. Jackson. And both he and Grandfather burst out laughing.

When the ponies were made comfortable, Nicky and Grandfather went to the nearest phone booth. Grandfather made the call. "Hello, Amanda," he said, "it's Father. I have someone who wants to talk to you in a minute, but I wanted to tell you first that we're all through here. We'll be loading up shortly and coming home. Now I'll turn you over to Nicky."

Nicky took the phone. "Mom?" he said.

"Hello, dear," said his mother. "Tell me — how did it go?"

Nicky took a deep breath. "Well," he said, "Guinevere won her class and then she went Show Champion Mare and then she won–the–Grand–Championship–and–the–Cymru–Cup!"

There was silence on the phone for a minute. Then Mrs. Davis said, "She *what?*"

"She won the Grand Championship and the Cymru Cup," said Nicky, more slowly this time.

Mrs. Davis gasped. "Oh, Nicky!" she cried. "How wonderful! How proud you must be! And how proud Grandfather must be."

"I am," said Nicky, and as he looked at Grandfather's face, he added, "and I think he is too."

"Well, we'll be in a fidget here till you get home and

can tell us all about it from beginning to end," said Mrs. Davis. "Good-by, darling. Have a good trip home. And give my love to our auction pony."

"I will," said Nicky. "You bet I will." And he slowly hung up the phone.

Epilogue

1963 Rule Book — American Horse Shows Association

Rule XXXI – Welsh Pony Division, Section 4

Type and Conformation. General Character: hardy, spirited and pony-like.

Any color except piebald and skewbald; head small and clean-cut, well set on and tapering to the muzzle, a slight dish is desirable; eyes bold, set wide apart; ears well-placed, small and pointed, well up on head; nostrils prominent; jaws and throat clean and finely cut. Neck shall be lengthy, well-carried and moderately lean in the case of mares, but inclined to be cresty in the case of stallions; shoulders long and sloping well back; withers moderately fine but not "knifey," the humerus upright so that the foreleg is not set in under the body. Forelegs should be set square and true, not tied in at the knees, with long, strong forearms, well-developed knee and short flat bone below. Back and loins should be muscular, strong and well-coupled; girth deep and ribs well-sprung; hind quarters lengthy and fine, not cobby, ragged or goose-rumped, with tail well set on and carried gaily; the hind legs should have large hocks, flat and clean with points prominent, to turn neither inwards nor outwards, the hind legs not to be bent, hocks not to be set behind a line from the point of the quarter to the fetlock joint. Pasterns should have medium slope and length, feet well-shaped and round, hoofs dense.